Mary Ashley Townsend

Down the Bayou and Other Poems

Mary Ashley Townsend

Down the Bayou and Other Poems

ISBN/EAN: 9783744708043

Printed in Europe, USA, Canada, Australia, Japan

Cover: Foto ©Andreas Hilbeck / pixelio.de

More available books at **www.hansebooks.com**

TO

OLIVER WENDELL HOLMES.

———◦◦———

To thee, whose home is in a nation's heart,
These little songs that I have dared to sing,
With tender love and reverence I bring, —
As one a flower might proffer and depart
Whence Wealth, Devotion, Beauty, Pride, and Art
Have proudly lavished many a worthier thing,
Due unto one who acts his noble part
In life's great drama with true rendering.
Would what I bring were many times more fair,
More worthy of thy genius and thy fame ;
Thy sweet, brave nature, thy attempered wit,
The clustering honors it is thine to wear,
And worthier far of thy illustrious name,
Which doth illume the page whereon 't is writ!

CONTENTS.

CONTENTS. 7

DOWN THE BAYOU.

WE drifted down the long lagoon,
My Love, my Summer Love and I,
Far out of sight of all the town,
The old Cathedral sinking down,
With spire and cross, from view below
The borders of St. John's bayou,
As toward the ancient Spanish Fort,
With steady prow and helm a-port,
We drifted down, my Love and I,
Beneath an azure April sky,
My Love and I, my Love and I,
    Just at the hour of noon.

We drifted down, and drifted down,
My Love, my Summer Love and I,
Beyond the Creole part of town,
Its red-tiled roofs, its stucco walls,
Its belfries, with their sweet bell-calls ;
The Bishop's Palace, which enshrines
Such memories of the Ursulines ;
Past balconies where maidens dreamed
Behind the shelter of cool vines ;

1*

Past open doors where parrots screamed ;
Past courts where mingled shade and glare
Fell through pomegranate boughs, to where
The turbaned negress, drowsy grown,
Sat nodding in her ample chair ;
Beyond the joyance and the stress,
Beyond the greater and the less,
Beyond the tiresome noonday town,
The parish prison's cupolas,
The bridges, with their creaking draws,
And many a convent's frown, —
We drifted on, my Love and I,
Beneath the semi-tropic sky,
While from the clock-towers in the town
Spake the meridian bells that said, —

> 'T was morn — 't is noon —
> Time flies — and soon
> Night follows noon.
> Prepare !   Beware !
> Take care !   Take care !
> For soon — so soon —
> Night follows noon, —
> Dark night the noon, —
> Noon ! noon ! noon ! noon !

To right, to left, the tiller turned,
In all its gaud, our painted prow.
Bend after bend our light keel spurned,
For sinuously the bayou's low
Dark waters 'neath the sunshine burned.

There, in that smiling southern noon,
As if some giant serpent, wound
Along the lush and mellow ground
To mark the path we chose to go ·
When, in sweet hours remembered now,
The long lagoon we drifted down;
My Love, my Summer Love and I,
Far out of reach of all the town,
Beyond the Ridge of Metairie,
And all its marble villages
Thronged with their hosts of Deaf and **Dumb**,
Who, to the feet of Death have come
And laid their earthly burdens down!

We drifted slow, we drifted fast,
Bulrush and reed and blossom past,
My Love, my Summer Love and I.
As the chameleon pillages
Its tint from turf, or leaf, or stone,
Or flower it haps to rest upon,
So did our hearts, that joyous day,
From every beauty in our way
Some new fresh tinge of beauty take,
Some added gladness make our own
From things familiar yet unknown.

With scarce the lifting of an oar,
We lightly swept from shore to shore, —
The hither and the thither shore,
With scarce the lifting of an oar, —

While far beyond, in distance wrapped,
The city's lines lay faintly mapped, —
Its antique courts, its levee's throngs,
Its rattling floats, its boatmen's songs,
Its lowly and its lofty roofs,
Its tramp of men, its beat of hoofs,
Its scenes of peace, its brief alarms,
Its narrow streets, its old *Place d'Armes*,
Whose tragic soil of long ago
Now sees the modern roses blow :
All these in one vast cloud were wound,
Of blurred and fainting sight and sound,
As on we swept, my Love and I,
Beneath the April sky together,
In all the bloomy April weather, —
My Love, my Summer Love and I,
In all the blue and amber weather.

We passed the marsh where pewits sung,
My Love, my Summer Love and I :
We passed the reeds and brakes among,
Beneath the smilax vines we swung ;
We grasped at lilies whitely drooping
Mid the rank growth of grass and sedge,
Or bending toward the water's edge,
As for their own reflection stooping.
Then talked we of the legend old,
Wherein Narcissus' fate is told ;
And turned from that to grander story
Of heroed past or modern glory.

Till the quaint town of New Orleans,
Its Spanish and its French demesnes,
Like some vague mirage of the mind,
In Memory's cloudlands lay defined ;
And back and backward seemed to creep
Commerce, with all her tangled tongues,
Till Silence smote her lusty lungs,
And Distance lulled Discord to sleep.

We drifted down, and drifted down,
My Love, my Summer Love and I.
The wild bee sought the shadowed flower,
Yet wet with morning's dewy dower,
While here and there across the stream
A daring vine its frail bridge builded,
As fair, as fragile as some dream
Which Hope with hollow hand hath gilded.
Now here, now there, some fisher's boat,
By trudging fisher towed, would float
Toward the town beyond our eyes ;
The drowsy steersman in the sun,
Chanting meanwhile, in drowsy tone, —
Under the smiling April skies,
To which the earth smiled back replies, —
Beside his helm some barcarole,
Or, in the common patois known
To such as he before his day,
Sang out some gay *chanson créole*,
And held his bark upon its way.

Slowly along the old shell road
Some aged negro, 'neath his load
Of gathered moss and *latanier*
Went shuffling on his homeward way;
While purple, cool, beneath the blue
Of that hot noontide, bravely smiled,
With bright and iridescent hue.
Whole acres of the blue-flag flower,
The breathy Iris, sweet and wild,
That floral savage unsubdued,
The gypsy April's gypsy child.

Now from some point of weedy shore
An Indian woman darts before
The light bow of our idle boat,
In which, like figures in a dream,
My Love, my Summer Love and I,
Adown the sluggish bayou float;
While she, in whose still face we see
Traits of a chieftain ancestry,
Paddles her pirogue down the stream
Swiftly, and with the flexile grace
Of some dusk Dian in the chase.

As nears our boat the tangled shore,
Where the wild mango weaves its boughs,
And early willows stoop their hair
To meet the sullen bayou's kiss;
Where the luxuriant " creeper" throws
Its eager clasp round rough and fair

To climb toward the coming June ;
Where the sly serpent's sudden hiss
Startles sometimes the drowsy noon, —
There the rude hut, banana-thatched,
Stands with its ever open door ;
Its yellow gourd hung up beside
The crippled crone who, half asleep,
In garments most grotesquely patched,
Grim watch and ward pretends to keep
Where there is naught to be denied.

The castled crayfish shows his tower,
Mud-built. half hidden in the weeds,
Above his deftly sunken well ;
And there the truant, in his hour
Of idle aims and wanton needs,
Will come with bit of scarlet bait,
And. loitering long. will patient wait
To drag the hermit from his cell.
Beside the bank we smile to hear
The breezy gossip of the plain
Come lightly to the listening ear ;
The rushes whisper to the cane,
The cane the spiked palmetto nears,
The grasses rustle as they tell,
Then runs the whisper back again,
As if the olden secret grew,
  As secrets will, both old and new,
That " Midas, he hath asses' ears."

The white clouds drifted overhead,
As on we passed, my Love and I ;
They sailed the sky like phantom ships
With phantom freight, — their port a dream,
Their course a careless idler's theme.
Across the lush and lonesome marsh
The heron's cry rose shrill and harsh ;
O'er distant plains the cattle wound
For noonday rest on shadowed ground ;
And now we talked, and now we read
The day-dream of some dreamer dead ;
Or, trailing there our finger-tips
In lazy tides our frail bark under,
Of heroes spoke with awe and wonder,
Or poets named of some far day,
Who had bequeathed unto our time,
In pages quaint of dolorous rhyme,
A heritage of youthful loves,
Which round their lives had seemed to play
As summer lightning plays round warm
Night-skies to which it brings no harm.
Then flocks of golden butterflies
Fluttered our painted prow before,
Seeming to draw us shore from shore.
The Love Queen's ribbon-guided doves,
Which, so the mythic legend proves,
Her chariot drew o'er roads of stars
Whereon her wheels have left no scars,
Were not more gorgeous in their dyes
Than our unharnessed butterflies ;

As yellow as if all their wings
Were made of golden wedding-rings,
And silent as if each were made
Of sweet things lovers leave unsaid.

Still darkly winding on before,
For half a dozen miles or more,
Past leagues and leagues of lilied marsh,
The murky bayou swerved and slid,
Was lost, and found itself again,
And yet again was quickly hid
Among the grasses of the plain.
As gazed we o'er the sedgy swerves,
The wild and weedy water curves,
Towards sheets of shining canvas spread
High o'er the lilies blue and red,
So low the shores on either hand,
The sloops seemed sailing on the land.

Now here, now there, among the sedge,
As drifted on my Love and I,
Were groups of idling negro girls,
Half hid behind the swaying hedge
Of wild rice nodding in the breeze.
Barefooted by the bayou's edge,
Just where the water swells and swirls,
They watched the passing of our boat.
Some stood like caryatides
With arms upraised to burdened heads ;
Some, idly grouped among the weeds,

B

With arms about their naked knees,
Or full length on the grasses cast,
Grew into pictures as we passed.
Our aimless course they idly noted,
Then out across the lowlands floated
Rude snatches of plantation songs,
In that sweet cadence which belongs
To their full-lipped, full-lungéd race.
We heard the rustle of the grass
They parted wide to see us pass ;
Our boat so neared their resting-place,
We heard their murmurs of surprise,
And glanced into their shining eyes ;
Then caught the rich, mellifluous strain
That fell and rose, and fell again ;
And listened, listened, till the last
Clear note was mingled with the past.

We drifted on, and drifted on,
My Love, my Summer Love and I.
All youth seemed like an April land,
All life seemed like a morning sky.
Like the white fervor of a star
That burns in twilight skies afar,
Between the azure of the day,
And gates that shut the night away ;
Bright as an Ophir jewel's gleam
On some Egyptian's swarthy hand,
About my heart one radiant dream
Shone with a glow intense, supreme,

Yet vague, withal, like some sweet sky
We trust for sunshine, nor know why.
The reed birds chippered in the reeds,   ·
As drifted on my Love and I ;
The sleepy saurian by the bank
Slid from his sunny log, and sank
Beneath the dank, luxuriant weeds
That lay upon the bayou's breast,
Like vernal argosies at rest.

Like some blind Homer of the wood, —
A king in beggared solitude, —
Upon the wide, palmettoed plain,
A giant cypress here and there
Stood in impoverished despair :
With leafless crown, with outstretched limbs,
With mien of woe, with voiceless hymns,
With mossy raiment, tattered, gray,
Waiting in dumb and sightless pain,
A model posing for Doré.
Aloft, on horizontal wing,
We saw the buzzard rock and swing ;
That sturdy sailor of the air,
Whose agile pinions have a grace
That prouder plumes might proudly wear,
And claim it for a kinglier race.

From distant oak-groves, sweet and strong,
The voicy mocking-bird gave song. —

That plagiarist whose note is known
As every bird's, yet all his own.
As shuttles of the Persian looms
Catch all of Nature's subtlest blooms,
Alike her bounty and her dole
To weave in one bewildering whole,
So has this subtile singer caught
All sweetest songs, and deftly wrought
Them into one entrancing score
From his rejoicing heart to pour.

Remembering that song, that sky,
" My Love," I say, " my Love and I " —
" My Summer Love " — yet know not why.
We had been friends, we still were friends ;
Where love begins and friendship ends,
To both was like some new strange shore
Which hesitating feet explore.
There had we met, surprised to meet
And glad to find surprise so sweet :
But not a word, nor sigh, nor token,
Nor tender word unconscious spoken,
Nor lingering clasp, nor sudden kiss,
Had shown Love born of Friendship's broken,
Golden, glorious chrysalis.

Each well content with each to dream,
We drifted down that silent stream,
Searching the book of Nature fair,
To find each other's picture there,

Lifting our eyes
To name the skies
Prophets of cloudless destinies,
As down and down the long lagoon
We swept that semi-tropic noon,
Each one as sure love lay below
The careless thoughts our lips might breathe,
Or lighter laughter might unfold,
As doth the earnest alchemist know
Beneath his trusted crucibles glow
Fires to transmute his dross to gold.

The wind was blowing from the south
When we had reached the bayou's mouth,
My Love, my Summer Love and I.
It laden came with rare perfumes, —
With spice of bays. and orange blooms,
And mossy odors from the glooms
Of cypress swamps. Now and again,
Upon the fair Lake Pontchartrain,
White sails went nodding to the main ;
And round about the painted hulls
Darted the sailing. swooping gulls,
Wailing and shrieking. as they flew
Unrestingly 'twixt blue and blue,
Like ghosts of drownèd mariners
Rising from deep sea sepulchres,
To warn, with weird and woful lips,
Who go down to the sea in ships.

We moored our boat beside the moat
Beneath the old Fort's crumbling wall.
No sudden drum gave warning sharp,
No martial order manned the Fort,
No watchful step the bastion smote,
No challenge from a sentry's throat
Sent down to us its questioning call.
No gleam of bayonet met the eye.
No banner broadened 'gainst the sky,
No clash of grounded arms was heard,
No ringing cheer. no murmured word,
No feet of armies marching by.
From moat and scarp and counterscarp,
From parapet to sally-port.
All lay untenanted and mute.
One grim, invisible sentinel,
Silence, gave to us sad salute,
Then died, as there our footsteps fell.

We climbed the ramparts, hand in hand,
My Love, my Summer Love and I.
There had the dumb, industrious moss
Woven its tapestries across
The ancient brickwork, with a touch
Like Love, which, loving, giveth much.
There, undisturbed, the lichen's slow,
Gray finger all the walls along
Had writ, in untranslated song,
Its history of the fair, low land,

Its courtly dames, its maidens fair,
Its men, brave, proud, and debonair,
Its romance and its chivalry,
As known a hundred years ago.

Softly the fragrant southern breeze
From o'er the Mexic Gulf blew on,
Stirring the blossomed orange-trees,
And leafless groves of the pecan.
O'er crumbling paths we laughing went,
My Love, my Summer Love and I,
Or o'er the hidden trenches bent,
And lingered with a vague content
On bastion and on battlement.
There were the cannon, blear and black,
Directed toward no foeman's track ;
Swart battle's puny infants swung
In the rude cradle of a time
When dreams were dwarfs, invention young,
And science, with its white, sublime,
Eternal face, yet scarcely free
From swaddles of its infancy.
With deep throats void of even a threat,
Prone on the grass-grown parapet
In mute impotency they lay.
Up to the rigid mouth of one
A clambering rose its way had spun :
Freighting the air with sweet increase
Of fragrance, lavished near and far,

It clung there, like a kiss of Peace
On the barbaric lips of War.
With reverent hands we touched the strange,
Mute relics, that so sternly spake
Of strides that make the nations quake
With awe before the march of change.
To what might be, from what had been,
Our thoughts o'er luminous courses swept,
Till every boundary they o'erleapt
That marks the untried and unseen.
Then Doubt from her chill cloisters crept,
Surrendering unto Progress there
The rusting keys of all the realms
Dominioned by the dwarf, Despair;
And, wondering, conquered, awed, and dumb,
She gazéd toward the Yet to Come.

Like one some gladness overwhelms,
Till, in the joy with which 'tis rife
Is drowned all dread of chancing grief,
I laughed, I dreamed, that sunny day,
And bound in one full fragrant sheaf
The goldenest harvests of my life.

And now, whene'er an April sky
Bends o'er me like some vast blue bell;
When piping birds are in the reeds,
And earth is fed on last year's seeds;
When newly is the live-oak's tent
With tender green and gray besprent;

When wailing gulls are on the lake,
And woods are fair for April's sake;
When grassy plains their secrets tell,
And lilies with white wonder look
At other lilies by the brook;
When thrills the wild rice in the wind,
And cries the heron shrill and harsh
Along the lush and lonely marsh;
When in the grove the mocker sings,
And earth seems full of new-made things,
And Nature to all youth is kind, —
Once more, as in a vision, seem
To rise before me lake and stream;
Once more a semi-tropic noon,
A boat upon a long lagoon;
Two figures there, as in a dream,
Come, strangely dear and strangely nigh,
To touch me, and to pass me by.
And, as they pass, once more I seem
To see, beneath the April sky,
In all the blue and silver weather,
My Love, my Summer Love and I,
Drift down the long lagoon together!

2

"LE ROI EST MORT."

L IGHT all the lamps
    In the temples of the skies ;
Keep them trimmed and burning ;
    In extremis lies
        The Year.
Watch by the corpse, Arcturus, when he dies !

    Bid them all hither,
  The congregations of stars,
  Their high-priests and sages,
    Their crowned kings and czars.
      The Year
Is dead ; Uranus, vigil keep, and Mars !

    He has gone.hence
  From the palaces of Time —
  Hark ! for the royal sleeper
  How the planets chime ;
    While Earth,
Chief mourner, mourns the King dead in his prime.

Under the dome
Of midnight carry his bier.
Come, ye constellations,
    Gaze on him shrouded here ;
    Each thread
Of his winding-sheet is a human smile or a tear.

    Swing o'er his bed
Those hopes and fruitless schemes,
Those vain evanishings,
    That drift of dreams
    Called LIFE !
Alcyone, light the censer with thy beams !

    His cold, cold couch
Lies frosty under the moon ;
Weep, ye gentle Pleiades !
    Lyra's harp in tune
    Shall keep
Time to your tears for the King dead so soon.

    How pale he lies
In the shadowy aisle of Time !
In the catafalque of Ages
    Silently sublime
    He sleeps.
Ye stars ! chant together as in Creation's prime.

Bear forth the dead,
.   Through the valleys of the skies,
To far sidereal regions
Where lone and solemn lies
The Past, —
That vault whose gate Memory guards and glorifies.

Farewell, dead King,
Into whose treasury poured
The hopes and fears of millions:
Hide thou thy hoard
Within
The mystic sanctuaries of The Unrestored!

ST. JULIENNE.

A RARE and radiant girlish face,
    Touched with a tender, saintly grace ;

A brow of meekly proud reserve,
Sign of a cross on its patient curve ;

Her locks the hue of rich, dead gold,
About an innocent forehead scrolled ;

Eyes whose opaline lustre beams,
Pure as a poet's holiest dreams ;

Cheek as a polished sea-shell fair,
Sweet lips, half laughter and half prayer ;

A smile exceeding sweet, and yet
Pained with the pang of some past regret ;

A soul that loftily soars and sighs,
  Yet leading Self to the sacrifice ;

A heart as noble as ever rung
Its truthfulness out on a truthful tongue

Silently suffering, brave to endure,
Patiently prayerful, prayerfully pure ;

Gifted, glorious, half divine,
A heavenly soul in an earthly shrine,

By women praised, and adored by men,
Radiant, rare ST. JULIENNE!

ASHMED, THE RHYMER.

HE strode before the world and audience claimed;
It spurned him as unheralded, unfamed,
And sent him from its presence bowed, ashamed.

He turned, like one wrong cannot render meek,
And said, as burned the world's blow on his cheek,
" Yet will I come; men yet will hear me speak!"

Swept the swift years. They had forgot each other,
As friend doth friend forget, and brother brother;
The world, the poet, knew not one another.

Then one day, swiftly, like a rocket's flame,
A poet's thought went up the sky of Fame,
And lo! men clamored for the poet's name.

Ashmed, the rhymer, raised his head and heard.
Within his bosom something wistful stirred;
But silent stood he, uttering not a word.

"Poet," the world cried, "from thy hidden ways
Come forth; and be thou crowned with poet's bays!
Fame waits to name thee with impassioned praise."

Still Ashmed listened, muttering, "If one strong,
True voice hath aided Right, or silenced Wrong,
'T is well; what matters it who sung the song?

"'T is after all the kingdom, not the king;
Not seasons, but the harvest seasons bring;
Not poets, but the songs that poets sing.

"And worthless is the thing that men call fame,
And frail the bar 'twixt glory and 'twixt shame,
Frail that ephemeral shadow called 'a name.'

"Greatness may come to those who sit in state,
And glory unto them who 'stand and wait.'
Naught comes to him for whom *all comes too late!*"

Then he, like one of sore temptation rid,
Back to his cell with monkish footsteps slid;
And from the whole world Ashmed's face was hid.

"RECUÉRDO!"

"*RECUÉRDO!*" *si, amigo!*
    Sweet remembrance bears me far,
Where the Toltec temples crumble,
    Where the Aztec ruins are,
Where the broad banana's banner
    Droops above the bamboo hut,
Where the plumy palm-tree presses
    To its heart the milky nut.

" *Recuérdo!* " at the magic
    Music of your Mexic word,
How my pulses beat within me,
    How my heart is thrilled and stirred!
At its soft, syllabic murmur,
    Strange enchantment round me falls ;
And again I see the moonlight
    Gleam on Montezuma's halls ;

And I see the Indian children
    Play beneath the mango-trees,
While the breath of orange orchards
    Scents the palpitating breeze ;

2*   c

And I hear the clank of sabres,
  And the mustang's eager neigh,
As the mounted guard dash briskly
  Down the desolate highway.

Icy-bearded *Orizaba*,
  Clothed in snow and crowned with cloud;
White and mute *Iztaccihuatl*,
  Slumbering in her frozen shroud;
Cordova's fair coffee forests,
  Cerro del Becerro's height,
Many-meadowed Metla lying
  In her valley of delight;

Skies that arch in matchless splendor
  Matchless plains that lie below;
Marble hills that grandly girdle
  Marble-mansioned Mexico;
White-cathedralled Guadalupe,
  Cortez's *Trista Noche* camp. —
Rise, as rose Aladdin's palace,
  By the rubbing of his lamp;

And I see beside the fountains
  Dusky maidens smile and nod,
While I tread the ancient courtways
  Which the Aztec Emperor trod.
And the *Caballeros* gayly
  Laugh, and, laughing, gayly ride
Down the path where Guatimozin
  Turned upon his foes and died.

All adown the *Rio Chalco*,
    From the islanded lagoon,
Indian barges wander slowly
    In the amethystine noon ;
Brown canoes with scarlet poppies
    From the floating gardens float,
While some native minstrel lightly
    Strikes the Bandalone's note.

Yonder, by the ruined arches,
    And along the convent walls,
Picturesque where all is picture,
    An unfriended beggar crawls ;
Where Chapultepec's grim castle
    Its defiant shadow flings,
Halts the wretch whose veins inherit
    Blood, mayhap, that warmed its kings.

" *Recuérdo!* " si, *amigo!*
    Sweet remembrance bears me far,
Where the Toltec temples perish,
    Where the Aztec's idols are.
" *Recuérdo!* " at that whisper
    What glad echoes are recaught,
What mnemonic worlds are moulded
    From the nebulæ of thought !

THE SWIMMER.

G OLDEN-BEARDED and sunny-haired,
Strength in each knotted muscle laired,
Ivory-limbed, on the bold headland,
A breathing statue, behold him stand!

A leap, a plunge, and the foamy flood
Clasps to its breast the laughing blood,
While the pliant arms like marble shine
In the bold embrace of the buoyant brine.

Down, where shudder the cold seaweeds,
To pastures where the porpoise feeds,
Where the drum-fish beats his mystic drum,
And the silver mullet glides shy and dumb;

Up, to the light, on the breezy billow,
The wave his couch, and its crest his pillow;
To dive, to float, to sink, to swim,
Delight in each luxurious limb!

Stroke on stroke, now away, away —
Swimmer and billow both at play ;
While sea nymphs blend, with fingers weird,
The green of the wave with the gold of his beard.

Upward now is his bare, broad breast,
Stretched on the wave he lies at rest ;
Over his forehead the waters dip,
And lave the smile on his swarthy lip.

Swift-winged curlews swim the air,
Clouds creep out of their lofty lair ;
While now on the wave, now on the wing,
The sea-gull screams like a human thing.

Once and again, with an agile grace,
He to the wave turns his ruddy face ;
The soft, sweet wind blows out of the south,
And lifts the brine to his bearded mouth.

Parting the billows on either hand,
Glowing and dripping, he gains the land ;
Shakes from his locks and limbs the dew,
Wrings his beard, and is gone from view.

UPON THE PEAKS.

I STAND and gaze, from Shenandoah's height, —
  The western sun goes grandly to his doom ;
Day masks herself as the gray nun, Twilight,
  Weaves weird garments upon sunset's loom.
The pyramidic pines uprear their heads,
  Crowned with their crowns of everlasting green,
While o'er the mountain top the young moon sheds
  Her mellow glory on the silent scene !

Within the cedar copse the partridge beats
  A fond recall upon his mystic drum.
To paint the dying year in her retreats,
  In russet gown has sombre Autumn come.
The hectic flush is on the maple's cheek,
  A sallow hue the homely hickory wears, —
Some favor in the artist's eye to seek,
  Her graceful limbs the slender sapling bares.

The timid pigeon folds her dusky wings
  Within the shadow of the woody way ;

Beyond the chirring squirrel chattering springs
  To lead the eager hunter far astray.
The lonely whip-poor-will's unanswered note
  In iterant cadence thrills from yonder wood,
Like human yearnings that around us float,
  Acknowledged, felt, yet never understood.

The rattlesnake among the brushwood winds,
  A sightless wanderer in these autumn days;
The cooling streamlet he by instinct finds,
  Then coils beneath the dogwood's crimson blaze.
The wild clematis, prone to toy and tease,
  Her white cap tosses archly to the wind;
Then, like a hoyden, climbs the naked trees
  With witching grace, half savage, half refined.

In ruins lie the mighty oaks and pines,
  By time hewn down a hundred years agone, —
Proud columns torn from nature's solemn shrines,
  To crumble here unmourned, unmissed, unknown.
The wintry winds rush o'er them unrestrained,
  The lichen wraps them in its velvet shroud, —
By mortal touch their grandeur unprofaned,
  By mortal hand their majesty unbowed.

Wave after wave, the hills their heads uprear;
  Afar, the billowy mountains boldly rise,
Like waters checked in full and mad career,
  Toward the blue illimitable skies;

In motionless magnificence they stand,
    The azure peak, the undulating hill, —
Wild seas to which, in gentle reprimand,
    The voice of Christ has murmured, " Peace, be still ! "

What, to the seal of all-transcendent Power
    Here stamped on crag, and rock, and rent abyss,
Was ancient Babylon in her happiest hour,
    Or Thebes, or Tyre, or proud Persepolis? —
What were Palmyra's palaces to these?
    Her sculptured fanes to such God-written pages, —
These mountain kings of mountain monarchies,
    These sage instructors of the proudest sages?

Ye hoary peaks ! ye proud exulting heights !
    Ye stony sponsors for the passing years !
For you Time hath no changes, Death no blights,
    And Life no mildew, misery, nor tears.
The solemn centuries, marching to the tomb
    In changing ranks, unchanging will ye see ;
Till clashing cycles toll the hour of doom,
    That merges Time into Eternity.

LOST AND FOUND.

L OST! a sunny-featured child,
Winsome, wayward, loving, wild, —
Blooming cheeks and amber tresses,
Lisping speech and sweet caresses ;
    Lost, lost, lost. lost!
      Have her feet thy pathway crossed?

Lost! oh, listen! lost! a child,
Fair, and dear, and undefiled ;
Lost! all those unworded blisses
Garnered in a baby's kisses ;
    Lost, lost, lost, lost!
      Spare her, world! thy fire, thy frost!

Coaxing lips and stainless brow,
Eyes like violets under snow,
Dimples, where the Witch of Laughter
Hid, and drew the roses after ;
    Lost, lost, lost, lost!
      Winds! where are her tresses tossed?

Child, such as the artist saint,
Raffaelle Sanzio, loved to paint,
When he put in angel places
Little, happy, human faces;
　　Lost, lost, lost, lost!
　　Seas, hath she your billows crossed?

Who will bring my darling back
To my desolate life track, —
Back with all her wayward winning,
Artless arts, and sinless sinning?
　　Lost, lost, lost, lost!
　　Earth, hath she thy boundaries crossed?

————

FOUND.

—

FOUND! a maiden tall and slender, —
　　Eyes of strange, magnetic splendor;
Lips, whose coaxing crimson teaches
To my heart its tenderest speeches;
Hands that lie to-day in mine,
Pilgrims resting at a shrine;
Calm, courageous, girlish mouth;
Breath as sweet as zephyrs south

Which, o'er brake and over brine,
Bear orange scents and jessamine.
Mingled with a rare discreetness,
Hath she fascinating sweetness ;
With a woman's soul intense
Linked a child's fresh confidence.
Found ! whose baby locks I curled, —
Found, " unspotted from the world," —
   Found, found, found, found,
    Whom I sought the earth around !

All the witching arrogance
Of happiness her charms enhance ;
In her lithesome, leopard grace
Lies a rare ancestral trace ;
In the pose of her young head,
Pride and gentleness inbred ;
In her gestures, free from guile,
In her glance, and in her smile,
Lightly lies the fact disguised.
The woman has the child surprised !
All my lost one's curls are there,
In her braids of golden hair ;
All my little one's caresses
In the maiden's gentle kisses ;
All of childhood's better part
In the maiden's warm, young heart.
   Found, found, found, found !
   Hath the earth a gladder sound ?

Found! oh, hear me! found! a woman —
Most angelically human ;
All the child's imperfect sweetness
Rounded to a rare completeness.
Worldly evil — deed nor word —
Never from her brow has stirred
The white, white bird of innocence
Resting there with reverence.
Infancy has dowered her youth
With its pureness and its truth.
On the ills that round her be,
Falls her sunny charity.
At the candor of her lips
Falsehood shudders in eclipse.
Living for exalted aims,
True to all life's noblest claims,
   I have found her — undefiled,
   In the woman all the child!

L'AMOUR.

I SEARCHED the garden of my heart,
　　And found a strange flower there ;
　　Its breath was sweet
　　In the lone retreat,
　　　And its mystic face
　　　Illumined the place,
Where from other blossoms it bloomed apart.

I touched its petals bright and rare,
　　And said, " Whence art thou, O flower?
　　A wondrous grace
　　I see in thy face ;
　　　Take root in my heart,
　　　For no more we part " —
Came the chilling whisper, " Beware ! beware ! "

I smiled and bent the bloom above ;
　　" Who warneth me thus? " I said.
　　" I am blessing and blight,
　　I am pain and delight,

I am drought and dew,
I am Laurel and Rue,
I am all things in one; my name is Love!"

With joy supreme my soul was rife;
I gathered and wear the flower:
It is blessing and balm,
It is rapture and calm,
It is wisdom and truth,
It is beauty and youth,
And ermine, and sceptre, and crown of life!

CARNIVAL SONG.

L ONG live the King! shout, one and all! —
Long live the King of the Carnival,
  The King and his merry Court!
Greet him with shout, and cheer, and song,
For oh! life's Lenten days are long,
  Its Carnival is short.

Long live the King! though brief may be
His regal pomp and pageantry;
  Some good must follow after
A sway unblemished by a tear,
A rule unclouded by a care, —
  One royal reign of laughter!

His name is heard in every hall;
His banner floats from every wall,
  Like some benignant pinion
Which in its royal plumage bears
Respite to all from one day's cares
  Throughout the King's dominion.

Most sovereign Grace! an easy thing
It is for any crownéd king
   To set Grief's tear-drops running;
Thine aim, to grant to every lip
From pleasure's bowl one harmless sip,
   Requires more dexterous cunning.

Rejoice, O Sire! that thine it is
To add some mite to human bliss,
   To make some lives the brighter.
How few can say that for one day
The world was happier for their sway,
   One single heart the lighter!

May every subject bend the knee
In glad allegiance unto thee,
   O King of fun and folly!
The old be young, the young be gay,
The brown locks mingle with the gray,
   And all the world be jolly.

What though the snow be on the hair,
And all be dim, once debonair,
   The heart grows agéd never;
Its sap is the sap of the evergreen,
And 'neath thy sceptre's magic sheen
   Will flow as fresh as ever.

Then live the King! shout, one and all!
Long live the King of the Carnival!
   Greet him with shout and song.
All hail, the King and his merry Court!
For oh! life's Carnival is short,
   Its Lenten season long.

LOUISIANA TO MASSACHUSETTS.

THROUGH the ambient spaces swinging, hark,
  Comes a voice of welcome ringing! Dark
And heavy has my heart lain broken, while
It longed for one such token, one such smile,
             Massachusetts!

I have bowed in dust and ashes, scarred
Foully by defiling lashes, marred
By those who, in my proud and palmy days,
Loved best to twine my balmy wreath of bays,
             Massachusetts.

I have drooped, despised in anguish, — yea.
Foes have laughed to see me languish; they
Have cursed me, scourged me, and upbraided — gods!
I lay unarmed, unaided 'neath their rods,
             Massachusetts!

But, in hours of my unsparing woe,
Flood and Famine at me staring, — lo!

I, groping helpless, faint and gasping, there
A hand felt clasping mine in my despair,
                    Massachusetts!

And that hand poured forth its treasure, fair,
Golden, without stint or measure, where
It fed and feeds like heavenly manna yet,
And Louisiana never can forget
                    Massachusetts.

From thy hearth was caught the ember brand
Which fired the souls of my September band;
My martyred heroes rushed to battle then,
And Concord's musket-rattle rang again,
                    Massachusetts!

Sisters, from one sire descended, we
Tyrants' chains alike have rended.   See!
Louisiana, wronged, blasphemed, undone,
Now free, redeemed, responds to Lexington,
                    Massachusetts.

NEW ORLEANS, Nov. 29, 1874.

THEY SAY.

THEY say 't is perfect weather; that the days
  Are strangely lovely, and the long nights fair;
That down the lanes the laughing Autumn comes
  With purple asters in her golden hair.
They say her slender feet are hid in bloom,
  That in her crown the golden-rod is glad;
In scarfs of wild peas and of passion-vines,
  They say her form is beautifully clad.

They say the forests never were so fair;
  The distant skies, they say, were never bluer;
And they that clasp hands send a whisper down,
  To say that never yet were true hearts truer.
They say the white waves on the scrollèd beach
  Sing to the white stars in the clear night sky;
They say the pine-tree on the sandy shore
  Is Summer's harp, on which she chants " Good-by."

They say the late bird, in the orange-boughs,
  Fills with a music shower his leafy lair;
That each note, perfected by Summer's hand,
  Drops like a jewel through the yellow air.

For me, alas! for me, the late bird sings
  Of Summer hopes that lost themselves in calms,
And left me standing, with a starving heart,
  At Autumn's gates, with hands too proud for alms.

WILLIAM BARRON'S BALCONY,

TACUBAYA, MEXICO.

BENEATH my feet a wondrous garden lies.
So rich its mass of color, light, and shade,
Its blended tints, its contrast of rare hues,
'T is like the Persian's magic mat of old,
There waiting but the pressure of a foot,
The utterance of a wish, to bear one hence.

Chained unto Wealth's all-conquering chariot wheel,
Stand India's floral queens, and Afric's palms.
Beneath the frigid glitter of snow peaks
Fair tropic captives keep their native bloom,
In beauty's pride defying any fate.
Cedars are there, the rarest of their race,
Whose ancestors were great in Lebanon.
The Eucalyptus straightens its tall form
Until its head is reared so high in air
Men look in wonder at its lofty crown,
And one, a simple poet, says, " Perhaps
It hath a human longing in its heart,

And hastens upward, hoping for a height
From which it may behold its native home
In far-away Australia's sea-girt soil."

Among the shadows, labyrinthine walks
Beguile the feet toward enchanting groves ;
Toward caverns guarded by the graven gods
Which Aztec worshippers adored and feared ;
Toward grottos, formed so cunningly by man,
Nature herself claims credit of his work,
And smiling tells, in each delusive spot,
In chasm, cascade, dripping rock and gorge,
In broken paths and sudden dungeon glooms,
In rugged rift and briery opening,
" The height of art is all art to conceal."

Long lakes, in ferny borders framed, give back
The ▬▬▬▬▬ azure of the sky. Swimming swans
Grace the reflective waters, and the sound
Of tinkling fountains thrills the balmy air,
Just making silence audible.
                              Far beyond
The rare exotics and the perfect lawns,
Rises the rocky and historic height
On which, in quaint and picturesque grandeur, stands
The grand old castle of Chapultepec.
Beside the broad road winding at its base,
Among the antique baths and sculptures old,
Tower the giant cypress-trees which struck
Their first roots here in centuries unknown

To those they sheltered centuries ago.
Their boughs were mighty in the grand old days
When proud, imperious Montezuma loved
To gather 'neath them nobles of his Court,
And the dusk faces of his thousand wives.
Under their shelter Guatimozin stood,
The young, heroic, martyred Aztec Prince,
When conquering princes built the scorching fires
Under his faithful and unflinching feet.

Kings and their kingly races have passed on ;
But by the castle gates the cypresses,
Draped in their swinging scarfs of pendent moss,
Stand in their uncrowned kingliness calmly there,
Like gray-locked bards from Odin's ancient halls,
And proudly chant " the days of the years of the Past."

Gelid as polar ice, dumb as dumb death,
Upon the right, Iztaccihuatl soars.
Rigid and awful in a ghastly shroud,
She lies outstretched upon her lofty bier,
While round her stiffened throat, departing day
A scintillant gorget clasps of crimson light,
Smitten from anvils of the setting sun.

Beyond her, pallid Popocatepetl !
Autocrat of heights, upon whose head
The keen, censorious centuries have laid
No gray, rebuking finger of decay,

He lifts aloft his time-anointed brow
As radiantly serene, and smooth, and white
As some pure page which lies as yet unwrit
'Neath the Recording Angel's lifted hand.
Before his icy scrutiny lies spread
The vale of Anahuac, a palimpsest
Whereon the writing of to-day blots out
The occult hieroglyphs of yesterday.

So he beheld the coming of that race
Which peopled first these plains.   So he looked on
The hands that hewed their stones, and reared their mounds,
And builded up their temples.   So he read
Their lost, mysterious histories, and saw
The unrecorded splendors of their reign.
He keeps the secret of their graven gods,
Their altars, and their wild idolatries.
He knows whence came they, whither they have gone ;
And all which hungering savans yearn to know
He holds between his grim lips, telling naught.
He sees the arch outlast the architect,
The shrine survive its worshipper, the dome
Glitter undimmed above its builder's dust.
Himself the centre of the cyclone Change,
Mutations move him not.   Men come and go,
Science works its miracles, worlds revolve,
Battle and Famine crowd against each other,
The lance of Knowledge bears down Ignorance ;
But midst all changes he unchanging stands,
His foot on buried kingdoms, and his crown

3*

Shining upon the key that could unlock
The mystic portals of Antiquity.

Hushed as the hopes a lover dares not breathe,
Lest speech should break the magic of love's spell,
Fair and afar the vale of Mexico,
With its strange beauty and its wasted powers,
The eye rejoices, and the thought aggrieves.
'Neath Evening's stroking fingers, soothed and calm,
It lies among its fragrant shadows, like
Some Eastern Queen who indolently courts
Repose beneath the scented fan, slow-waved
Above her by some Odalisk's patient hand.

On every side the milky maguey grows,
Resting upon the soil like tufts of plumes
Which some despairing chieftain band of yore,
Suddenly sinking from existence, left
Behind to tell it was — and is no more.

Laden with bales of modern merchandise,
A troop of plodding donkeys yonder winds
Toward the dusty road that leads along
The arches of that ancient aqueduct
Which, to the eager lips of Cortez, brought
The cool, sweet waters from the rugged hills, —
A blessing from the hands he came to smite.

In middle distance, dark and motionless,
Against a ruined column dreamily

An Indian woman leans, with gaze that seems
Fixed on the faded glories of her tribe.
Close to her breast a slumbering child is held ;
Another stands half fidden in the garb
That picturesquely drapes the unconscious grace
Which is the mother's savage heritance.
So statuesque the form of each and all,
They seem a group chiselled in murk obsidian.

Fronting the eye, a league or more away,
On Tenochtitlan's site stands Mexico.
The splendid city of the splendid plain.
Its moss-grown domes, its ancient Moorish towers,
Its crumbling convents and its fountained courts,
Its palace portals and its time-stained gates,
Rise, where Tezcuco's waters once were blue,
And view this land of conquered conquerors.

The purple hills clasp hands around its walls,
The unrivalled skies pour their rich splendor down.
The sunset fades, and o'er the darkening plain,
Out from their tall towers, slow and mournfully
The solemn bells of the Cathedral peal !

THE SUMMER.

IT came with bloom,
And sweet perfume,
And brooksongs low and tender;
With pinks awake,
For Summer's sake,
And days and nights of splendor.
It came with birds,
And low of herds,
And youthful footsteps straying
Beyond the yields
Of harvest fields,
While farmer folk went haying.

Now Summer's dawn
And dusk are gone;
And Autumn winds come straying
Through lane and wood,
Where erst we stood
When farmer folk went haying.

But all it brought,
And all it taught,
That Summer mid the mowing,
And what was said,
While cheeks grew red, —
What would ye give for knowing?

FLORA McDONALD.

DEAD in the morgue there, nobody claiming her,
  Nobody watching beside the young head,
Nobody missing her, nobody naming her,
  Nobody mourning because she is dead.

Out in the night-wind the street lamps flare wearily,
  Autumn leaves down from their branches are whirled;
Yonder, with dead eyelids folded down drearily,
  Poor human leaf drifted out of the world!

Nobody mourning her, no one so daring,
  Poor fragile wreck on life's desolate shore;
Only a Christ dares to share such despairing,
  Murmur forgiveness, and " Go, sin no more."

Youthful and fair once, white-souled and so winning,
  Pure as the purest that ever drew breath,
Fresh as a flower in its bud and beginning, —
  Love, with a kiss, stung its beauty to death!

Poor wretched heart, with no arms to enfold it,
  Cheated and wronged of its tenderest needs, —
Like some frail vine, with no good thing to hold it,
  Turning at last to entwine about weeds!

Out on life's stage to find all the crowd hissing her,
  Shuddering and striving to hide her poor face;
Reaching for aims that forever were missing her,
  Fainting and falling to shame and disgrace.

But in the morgue there is no more to worry her:
  Charity, Love, nor Uprightness draw near;
Too cleanly Purity e'en to help bury her,
  Virtue too holy to give her a tear.

Hark! comes a sound from the ranks unrespected,
  Murmur of voices — a woman's kind tone —
Saying, " 'T is shameful to leave her neglected,
  Friendless, forsaken, and dead here alone.

" Come ye here, women! Our fingers shall spin her
  Shroud white as any for saint in the land;
We are all sinners, — and she was a sinner, —
  Let her receive Christian rites at our hand.

" Poor murdered creature! our hearts know the aching,
  Love, turned a liar, can give with a sneer;
All of us know just what cruel forsaking
  Shattered this girl's life and hurried her here.

" Coffin her tenderly, shroud her all whitely,
   Twine ye the roses in cross and in crown ;
Place her tired feet and hands decently, rightly."
   So did these women there, — they " of the town."

They to that shrine in the morgue brought the preacher,
   Wept they for her whom nobody would own,
As fell the words of Christ Jesus, the Teacher,
   " Who without sin, let him cast the first stone."

So did they bury her, — they the unholy ;
   So did they give her their pity and care ;
So they wept for her, the lost and the lowly, —
   Won the deed no recognition Up There?

Aye ! on the page which the angel was smiting
   With sins of the Lost, a great glory swept down,
Setting across them in luminous writing
   This deed of the women there, — they " of the town."

MY LADY.

THERE she stands —
Looking along the low and level lands,
To where the sea's pulse beats upon the sands ;
A scarlet blossom in her quiet hands —

> My Lady !

Tall and fair,
Slender and pliant as young willows are ;
From arching foot to crown of braided hair,
Beauty's supreme and undisputed heir —

> My Lady !

Richer glows,
Her brow's immaculate ivory now shows ;
Dipped in a blush, Thought's tender pencil throws,
On each fair cheek, the warm light of a rose —

> My Lady !

Through the pines
An unexpected sunbeam slanting shines,
And, softening more the more that it declines,
The barren landscape brightens and refines

> Supremely.

E

Searching there,
It finds My Lady with her young head bare ;
And, stealing seaward, darts with regal care
A golden arrow through her golden hair —
My Lady !

Her gray eyes
Lift themselves upward, dreamy and cloud-wise,
To wander past aerial argosies,
And seek an eye-path to the sunset skies —
My Lady !

For she knows,
Toward the scaffold of the west there goes
Each eve a veiled young Day, who meekly bows
Beneath Time's sure and unrelenting blows —
My Lady !

She has stood
Oft and again, as now, in pensive mood
Between the salty sea and piny wood,
While the vast occident blazed with sunset's blood —
My Lady !

And the crime
Spilled its red splendor on the blue sublime,
And splashed the white stars with its crimson grime,
Until Night sponged it from the walls of time —
My Lady !

Now she stands,
And looks along the low and level lands
To where the still sky stoops to stiller sands;
The scarlet flower forgotten in her hands —
                    My Lady!

                    Oh for grace
. To paint the sweet, strange beauty of her face,
In whose exquisite lineaments I trace
The lordliest sigils of her lordly race —
                    My Lady!

                    A memory,
A dream of one fair dreamer by the sea,
In her unusual beauty she must be
Through all the future of my life to me —
                    My Lady!

                    Standing there,
She looks so pure, so marvellously fair,
She seems like some embodied Christian prayer
Which hastening angels seek to heavenward bear —
                    My Lady!

                    Yet I dare
To lay my soul where her feet resting are,
Believing she can lift it up afar,
Beyond the sunset, and the sunset star —
                    My Lady!

ASUNDER.

I MOURN!   O Love, what miles of sky,
   What weary, weary miles of sea,
Stretch out beneath, stretch out on high,
In maddening immensity,
   My darling one, 'twixt you and me!

Ten thousand pleasures lie between,
   Ten thousand thousand hearts of care ;
But whatsoever intervene,
For me one woe spans all the scene,
   That I am *here* and thou art *there.*

To Nature's feast of sweet perfumes,
   In saintly white and stainless union,
Come stealing forth from verdant glooms
The proud Magnolia's peerless blooms,
   Like virgins to their first Communion.

I look at them and think of thee,
   Thy perfect form, thy sinless face ;
How fair a flower thou art to me,
How sacred in the sanctity
   Of youthful beauty, pureness, grace !

Above the flowers I see the stars, —
　Those golden ships in azure seas,
With silent decks and shining spars,
Anchored beyond all earthly bars
　In the unknown eternities :

Still farther are those stars away
　Than thou, my darling, art from me ;
Yet, let mine eyes seek as they may,
To thee they cannot find their way
　Across the cruel land and sea !

But when Sleep's dusky hands surprise
　Mine eyes, no more we'll parted be ;
For Night, that jewelled bridge that lies
Between the sunset and sunrise,
　In dreams I'll cross and be with thee.

WHEN.

WHEN I am in my coffin laid,
  O Love! look not upon my face;
Let not so cold, so pale a thing
  Dreams of my living self replace.

The hands of ice, the cheek of snow,
  O'er which thy breath unheeded plays,
The idle pulse, the frozen veins,
  The eyes ungladdened by thy gaze;

The deafened ear, the lifeless lips,
  The brow of stone, the chilly hair,
The heart unmoved at thy approach, —
  What semblance of thy darling there?

Kiss me good-by while yet the throb
  Of sweet existence is my own;
While yet I thrill beneath thy lip,
  Yet drink the richness of thy tone!

While yet mine eyes can see in thine
   No look of anguish to deplore,
Kiss me good-by; then go thy way,
   And look upon my face no more:

Aye! go thy way, cast not a glance
   Again upon my drooping head;
Remember me as living, warm,
   And fair, and fond, and true; not — dead!

SONG.

MY little one, my little one,
  The blossom is not faded yet
You gave me once at set of sun,
  And whispered, " I will ne'er forget, —
            Will ne'er forget ! "

Its petals still their hues retain ;
  I touch it, and it crumbles not ;
I lay it on my heart again, —
  But, little one, thou hast forgot, —
            Thou hast forgot !

GUY'S GOLD.

NOT from the Western gulches,
    Nor Indian isles of old ;
Not from Peruvian gorges,
    Nor Russia's rigid hold,
Was gathered the wonderful treasure,
Was meted the bountiful measure, —
            Guy's Gold.

No opulent Mexic valleys,
    No Asian hillsides bold,
No Inca's brimming coffers,
    No miser hoards untold,
Were ever so rich as to render
This shimmering, scintillant splendor, —
            Guy's Gold.

There, in the ancient doorway,
    Guy sits ; the sun goes west ;
Suddenly o'er his shoulders,
    Suddenly o'er his breast,

4

Three happy young faces are beaming,
And over his bosom goes streaming
                    Guy's Gold.

Coronet, braid, and ringlet,
    Missing their ribboned hold,
Shining like summer moonlight,
    Untwist, uncurl, unfold.
Pressed deep in the turbulent tresses,
A hand fondly reverent blesses
                    Guy's Gold.

Down from each fair young forehead
    A dainty flower has rolled :
One is a red pomegranate,
    Blossom all fire and gold ;
One fragrant white jasmine had printed,
One deep-hearted lily had tinted,
                    Guy's Gold.

He lifts the falling flowers ;
    In them his fond eye traces
A vague, sweet symbolism
    Of all the joyous faces,
While over his shoulder is swinging,
And unto his bosom is clinging,
                    Guy's Gold.

Then laughter comes, and kisses,
  Girls' words in merry chase ;
While sweet, unwritten music
  Leaps out on Guy's glad face, —
Thanks God for the wealth he 's caressing,
Thanks God for that infinite blessing,
            Guy's Gold.

He close and closer clasps it, —
  Guinea, nor Ormus old,
E'er in auriferous caverns
  Held wealth that he doth hold, —
And, praying, he asks the All-Father
  To tenderly guard and to gather
            Guy's Gold ;

Prays that by day and night-time,
  Whate'er beguile or appall,
His hand be laid in kindness
  And mercy-love on all,
Until for Time's silver is bartered,
Until for high Heaven is chartered,
            Guy's Gold.

WHAT I SAW IN MY SLEEP.

I SAW a radiant woman stand
   Before me in my feverish dreams;
And her brow was white as a sea-sand drift
   On which the lightning gleams.

There was a glimpse of Heaven in her eye,
   A gleam of Hell in her yellow hair;
She was one of those angel fiends, I knew,
   That women sometimes are.

She spoke; her voice like a censer swung
   Perfumes on the palpitating air;
She had fed it, I knew, on the daintiest sweets
   In the Hadien *parterre*.

She had the tone of a dulcet bird,
   She deftly spoke with an adder's tongue;
And every enticing word she said,
   With serpent's poison stung.

Her sea-green eyes were fair to behold,
  And her crimson mouth was perfect lipped;
But out of her glance and out of her heart
  Invisible venom dripped.

I saw her lay her little white hand
  On trusting hearts of unsinning men;
And, after the thrill of that Circean touch,
  They ne'er were pure again!

I thought the flush on her burning cheeks
  Was bloom from happier worlds than this,
Till I dreamed in my dreams each round, red spot
  Was Satan's passionate kiss.

Then I knew she was some Plutonian spy,
  Sent from the sulphurous nether earth
To wake the tenderest passions of men,
  And poison them at birth.

So I hid myself from the woman's eyes,
  And muttered a hurried Christian prayer;
She vanished; but sometimes I see her yet,
  Miraculously fair!

IN DUBIO.

I SAT in the shade by a running river,
    And read a runic rhyme ;
While arrows of light, from the sun's full quiver,
Struck here and there with a scintillant shiver,
        Like shafts of flame
        Sent, wide of their aim,
    At the running target Time.

Away to the world went the river singing
       Its own mysterious lay.
A robin was earthward his music flinging,
His way o'er the meadows a plover was winging. '
        Ah ! life was sweet,
        And my pulses beat
    Time to youth's turbulent May.

Around and around on my finger, thinking,
       I turned a golden ring ;
From springs of the present my life was drinking,

From wells of the future my lips were shrinking;
  Turning astray
  From its noblest way,
  The heart is an aching thing!

" Thou'lt sit," said the Ring, " in earth's proudest places,
  And Pride is Love in disguise ;
Regret and Remorse will hide their dark faces
Forever, from paths which glad Opulence paces."
  O Sophistry,
  With thy mockery
  Stoning Truth to death with lies!

Still, hesitant, I of myself alone
  Dreamed midst God's vast creation,
And muttered, " I sin not ; gold shall atone
For life degraded, for love never known."
  The idle lives
  Of rich men's wives, —
  Were they my base temptation?

The voice of my soul whispered, " Cease thy dreaming ;
  Scorn what the tempter saith,
Else narrow thy life to a piteous seeming,
Engirdle thy days with a shameful scheming :
  A solemn thing
  Is a plain gold ring,
  And all it encompasseth."

Then seemed my heart-beats a multitude hasting
      My future to crucify ;
The apples of Sodom my young lips were tasting,
Yet kissed they the ashes on which they were wasting ;
            For the mean sake
            Of a glittering stake,
      Mortgaging life to a lie !

" Can woman accept. with its laws unbending,
      The narrow realm of the Ring ;
Be true to a falsehood that knows no ending,
Be false to a truth that her heart is rending,
            Yet hold her soul
            In such firm control,
      It never shall faint 'neath the sting ? "

I heard the voice while the river went sliding
      Its devious track along ;
With rugged places its beauty dividing,
Feeling its way where the cowslips were hiding,
            For better, for worse,
            True unto its course,
      Contentedly still and strong.

I saw on a rock, where the sunlight slanted,
      A serpent's fascinant coil ;
Its terrible beauty a bird enchanted,

Till deep in its bosom a fang was planted,
    With its selfish lust
    Laying dead in the dust
Its frail, bewildered spoil.

And I saw the prey of a vulture bleaching
    Its bones on a rocky shelf.
" Lo! Nature," I said, " is with symbols preaching ;
The tone of her wisdom I hear in her teaching,
    Saying to me,
    ' Undauntedly be
A woman true to herself!' "

Quick down in the deeps of the silent river
    I buried the ring of gold ;
Down under the current I saw it quiver ;
Its dazzling gleam with a drowning shiver
    Went out of my life,
    And left it all rife
With a woman's truth unsold.

   .   .   .   .   .   .

I gaze at the river rapidly running
    Above the silver mosses ;
At the creeper, its scarlet tankards sunning,
Yet the drowning dash of the ripples shunning ;
    At the graceful dip
    Of the lily's lip
To the gleam the water crosses.

I watch, while the evening cloud-lands vary
From gold to porphyry ;
From out of the blue floats an amber wherry,
An opal cloud o'er the sunset to ferry ;
And a single star
Has crossed the bar
Of Day, to Night's open sea.

Far o'er the hills is the sun descending,
The river slides to the sea ;
To a past unpoisoned is Memory bending,
To a joyous future my steps are tending, —
No golden bribe
Doth circumscribe
My soul's integrity.

CREED.

I BELIEVE if I should die,
  And you should kiss my eyelids when I lie
Cold, dead, and dumb to all the world contains,
The folded orbs would open at thy breath,
And, from its exile in the isles of death,
  Life would come gladly back along my veins.

I believe if I were dead,
And you upon my lifeless heart should tread,
  Not knowing what the poor clod chanced to be,
It would find sudden pulse beneath the touch
Of him it ever loved in life so much,
  And throb again, warm, tender, true to thee.

I believe if on my grave,
Hidden in woody deeps or by the wave,
  Your eyes should drop some warm tears of regret,
From every salty seed of your dear grief,
Some fair, sweet blossom would leap into leaf,
  To prove death could not make my love forget.

I believe if I should fade
Into those mystic realms where light is made,
   And you should long once more my face to see,
I would come forth upon the hills of night
And gather stars, like fagots, till thy sight,
   Led by their beacon blaze, fell full on me !

I believe my faith in thee,
Strong as my life, so nobly placed to be,
   I would as soon expect to see the sun
Fall like a dead king from his height sublime,
· His glory stricken from the throne of time,
   As thee unworth the worship thou hast won.

I believe who hath not loved
Hath half the sweetness of his life unproved ;
   Like one who, with the grape within his grasp,
Drops it with all its crimson juice unpressed,
And all its luscious sweetness left unguessed,
   Out from his careless and unheeding clasp.

I believe love, pure and true,
Is to the soul a sweet, immortal dew,
   That gems life's petals in its hours of dusk ;
The waiting angels see and recognize
The rich crown jewel, Love, of Paradise,
   When life falls from us like a withered husk.

TO THE MEXICAN EXILES.

FAR from these bland and balmy shores
    Your native peaks arise,
Saluting with their pallid lips
    Your bright, exultant skies.
There Popocatepetl puts
    Aside his crown of cloud,
And wears the snow from which was wrought
    Iztaccihuatl's shroud.

There, one by one, the stars step forth
    At gray-eyed twilight's beck,
And, helmeted in gold, stand guard
    Above Chapultepec.
The evening gales are scented with
    The sighs of sleeping flowers,
And, ghostlike, down the valley rise
    Old Guadalupe's towers.

La tierra caliente stands
    In sandals wrought of bloom, —
A red-lipped queen who. smiling, waves
    Her sceptre of perfume.

And from the palm and mango groves,
　The sweet *Cenzontle's* throat
Pours out its melody to meet
　The wild *Jilguero's* note.

There rise the shining palace walls,
　The convent's ancient dome;
The hills, the groves, the roofs, the shrines,
　Of sweet and sacred home!
What can our lakes, our streams, our plains,
　Fair though they be, bestow
On hearts that mourn the mountain peaks,
　The vales of Mexico?

The billowy gulf that rolls between
　Brings on its scrollèd waves
No kisses from the lips ye love,
　No voices of your braves!
Alas! no balm have we to heal
　The anguish of regret;
And here no Lethe rolls to teach
　The exile to forget.

But thought, the soul's fair carrier-dove,
　With free and unclipped wing,
Sent from the drifting ark of life,
　Back o'er the seas will bring
Some treasure of the olden time,
　Some flower that won your praise
Green memories of the land ye love,
　And dreams of happier days.

YOUR LETTER.

I KISSED your letter when it came,
　I clasped it in my throbbing palms ;
Tumultuous joy-storms swept my heart
　From out its olden summer calms.

The lily nodded to the rose,　·
　The rose in richer hues seemed clad ;
The skies put on a tenderer blue, —
　All things seemed glad that I was glad.

I broke in haste the shining seal,
　With quaint devices deftly wrought, —
The waxen lock that kept for me
　Words woven in the loom of thought.

"That royal loom !" I, smiling, said ;
　" Whence comes this texture, warp, and woof,
Each glowing, scintillating thread,
　Of Love's Golcondian wealth a proof?"

I read ; the glittering words were there, —
  Pearls, rubies, emeralds of thought,
Bright sapphire links, and diamond drops. —
  But where, oh ! where the love I sought?

Was this the letter I had prized,
  And blessed for falling to my lot?
True, much I found, but more I missed ;
  For what was *all* where love was not?

SCALLOP, and conch, and salt sea sand,
    A blue and boundless sky ;
White on his arm a little shy hand,
    Holding his destiny.

The cool wax-myrtle's mellow green,
    Brightening the marshy isles,
Sweet whispers softly uttered between
    A maiden's merry smiles.

An earnest man, a laughing girl,
    A stretch of sea-girt beach ;
A fluttering ribbon, a wind-tossed curl,
    A moment's trembling speech.

A fair face toward the far lagoon,
    A rose-red girlish mouth ;
The lighthouse tower in the blaze of noon,
    The warm wind from the south.

The rise and dip of dancing prows,
   A murmured " We must part ; "
The pencilled curve of two arching brows,
   A strong man's broken heart.

.   .   .   .   .

Scallop, and conch, and salt sea sand,
   A drift of cloudy sky.
The sob of waves on the shining strand,
   Ocean's immensity !

A heron white on the lone lagoon.
   Foam on the billow's crest ;
The lighthouse tower pale under the moon,
   The wild wind from the west.

The black sea-chestnut billow-strewn
   Along the lonely strand ;
A stony heart, whose tares were sown
   By some one's false white hand.

The lightman's lamp, a spark of gloom
   Amidst the gloomy dark ;
A soul that drifts to its desolate doom,
   A wrecked, dismantled bark.

.   .   .   .   .

Scallop, and conch, and salt sea sand,
   A drift of cloudy sky,
The sob of waves on the shining strand,
   Ocean's immensity !

HE AND SHE.

SHE said, " Take thou this rose, and let it be
For just one night a memory of me ;

" From out its petals if a dew-drop fall,
Some tear I've shed with thee let it recall.

" Read in its hues, caught from the perfect weather,
Some perfect joy we two have shared together.

" If from its depths rich odors sudden start,
Let them remind thee of a woman's heart,

" Which learned. in opening its depths to thee,
That love is life's most near necessity."

He said. " The rose thou offerest me I take,
To cherish ever for the giver's sake !

" To me a simple flower it cannot seem,
Nor vagrant blossom of a summer dream ;

" For all its precious petals make the sum
Of days bygone. of golden days to come.

" When its sweet beauty wins my tender praise,
Thy sweeter beauty will come back always.

" Forever and forever it shall sleep,
Where I my purest, holiest treasures keep."

.   .   .   .   .

They parted then.   She went and stood next day
Just where she gave her little rose away.

Her soul was filled with many a tender thought,
His sweet acceptance of the flower had brought.

She glanced about the half-disordered room.
Toward its planes of light, its nooks of gloom;

Then at some trifles idly thrown away,
Like toys thrown down by children tired of play;

A crumpled thing, its stainless beauty fled.
There, in their midst, her little rose lay dead!

DAME AILSIE.

"A PENNY for your thought," I smiling said,
    And touched with reverent hand Dame Ailsie's
      head.
Pale, proud Dame Ailsie, with the snow-white hair,
And face whose beauty still shines through its care.
New sorrows scarce can ever touch her more ;
The barks that held her treasures by the shore
Have all put out, and left her on life's sands,
A lonely mourner wringing empty hands.

Her neighborship to me is very dear ;
And often, on the winding stair of stone
That from the wide banquette leads to my door,
Of, but not in, the city's restless roar,
We meet, and hold our woman chats alone.
Or, as the balmy southern eve draws near,
On the quaint balcony, that hangs below
My dormer windows and the ancient eaves
Where little waifs of weeds and grasses grow,
And where his mossy monogram Time weaves

About the old brick chimneys, as to stay
The gnawing tooth of pitiless decay,
We draw our bamboo chairs, and, side by side,
Note the air-beating bat with sudden flight
From his day dungeon swiftly hastening
To quilt the widths of space with nervous wing;
Or watch the gray ship Dusk serenely glide
Across the fading sunset's outer bars
Into the blue and broadening gulf of night,
To drop her anchors in a sea of stars.

The rushing wheels of time with talk we clog,
As up behind the gray old synagogue
Which rears its Moorish towers just o'er the way,
The moon from far beyond the river rises,
And with strange splendor all the town surprises;
Across the uneven roofs, that intervene
'Twixt us and distant features of the scene,
We watch it with a wand of silent fire
Smite into radiance yon tapering spire,
While still beyond its opulent rays endower
The matchless grandeur of St. Patrick's tower.

Our eyes are earnest lovers of the skies.
Their clouds, their stars, their sunset and sunrise,
Their constant march of change, their light, their shade,
Their dusk of storms, their sunbursts; their dismayed
Blue acres of the air-farms, overflowed
With silent cataracts of rended cloud;

Their caverns where the thunder-steeds they keep,
And lightning whips to lash them if they sleep ;
The mystic gardens of the solemn night,
Sown dark miles deep with shining seeds of light ;
The constellations, as they sink and rise, —
Those untranslated gospels of the skies ;
The constant dying and the constant birth
Of variable things above the earth, —
All these our eyes delighted watch ; and oft
As we together turn our eyes aloft,
Searching the fathomless wonders of the dark
That enter into Night's stupendous ark,
All petty, worldly cares sink out of sight,
And leave us lonely with the Infinite.

Thus had we sat now for uncounted time,
Watching the sky-scape, mooned, starred, and sublime,
Which stretched beyond the city roofs away,
Pierced by its towers, and spires, and gables gray,
When from Dame Ailsie's lip a sigh I caught,
And softly said, " A penny for your thought."
Upon her gentle hand she leaned her head,
Looked far away, then answered me and said :

" I call to mind to-night a girl who died, —
Ah me ! what weary, weary years ago.
How I did pity her, and how I cried
Above her placid and encoffined brow !
I laid my fingers on the chilled, fair hair,
Which round her laughing face had loved to curl,

'And, weeping, wailing, and rebelling there
Above the shrouded bosom of the girl,
With aching heart, I cried aloud, 'Oh, why
Should one so beautiful, so happy, die?
Life is so rich, so bountiful a thing,
So full of flowers to pluck, of songs to sing,
Of joy and health, of beauty and of youth,
Of promise and fulfilment, love and truth, —
Why was she robbed of all?   Oh, why not spared
For yet a little while?'

             " Even as I dared
To murmur thus, her gravestone rose between
My anguished face, her coffined form serene,
Bearing the sculpture ' DIED AT SEVENTEEN !'

" Oh, what a piteous thing it seemed to me,
Her death and burial with life's spring so green !
How cruel the relentless, stern decree
Summed in those few words, ' *Died at seventeen !* '

" I too was young.   With white, unwounded feet
I stood in life's fresh lanes, and saw the sweet,
Enticing radiance by the future thrown
About the hill-tops of the Yet Unknown.
My hands were full of youth's unfaded flowers,
My lips were touching its untasted hours ;
Toward happy fields of rose and mignonette
My bounding heart and hopeful eyes were set :
Therefore I cried aloud, with faltering tongue,
' O God ! how sad a thing to die so young !'

" Ah, that was long years since. Sunshine and snow
Have fallen and faded many a time, I know,
Where once I wept above that slender grave,
And pitied her who unto dust we gave.
But now, to-night, with something that's akin
To envy, comes my heart's lone doors within
The memory of that slim, green grave afar,
Gemmed by the daisies, greened with gentle rain,
Free from life's fire, or fret, or passion's pain ;
And, as dumb Thought, a lonely pilgrim, goes
O'er blighted fields of mignonette and rose,
Afar, far off that dead girl's face appears :
I see it without sorrow, without tears,
And sigh, while gazing on the scarred Between,
' O God ! that I had died at seventeen ! '"

BY THE BIRD-CAGE.

SEEDS for thy banquet. my warbler,
    Flowers for thy palace of song —
Hush now ; my senses are weary,
    Thou hast sung loudly and long !
Into my presence a vision
    Came with thy last thrilling note,
Which, like a cadence elysian,
    Soared from thy marvellous throat.

Oh ! what I heard as it floated,
    Filtering its sweetness through sweets,
Born of the blooms of the orange
    Fringing these narrow old streets.
Oh ! what I felt as its sifted
    Tenderness fell through the flowers, —
How my soul drifted and drifted
    Back through life's beautiful hours !

Only the notes of a bird-song,
　Only a blossom sweet-scented ;
Only a touch unforgotten,
　Only a moment repented ;
Only a shallop that grounded,
　Where the deceiving sands lay
Hidden, and still, and unsounded,
　Out in life's beautiful bay !

From its wreck, lone and deserted,
　Just now a weird Presence stole,
And with its fragile hand sounded
　All the sad bells of my soul.
I, midst their chiming and flowing,
　Found the lost key to my fate :
Oh ! anguish, shaped out of knowing,
　When knowledge cometh too late !

Led by those little white fingers,
　Backward I'm borne to that shore
Where the dark waters are breaking
　Of the wild sea Nevermore.
'Gainst my sad heart they are beating,
　With their spray are mine eyes wet —
Hear them repeating, repeating,
　All that I never forget !

Once more I'm dreamily bending
  Over some intricate page ;
Sweetly a young voice is mingled
  With thine, O bird in the cage !
I see the mystical pages
  Swept by a maiden's bright curl ;
I read the lore of the sages.
  Read not the heart of a girl !

Curtains of white lace are swaying,
  Wanders the wind up and down ;
She by a window is sewing,
  In the old French part of town ;
Beams of the sunlight are golden,
  Pomegranate blossoms burn red ;
Dusky braids, many times folden,
  Crowning the young Creole head.

Up from the gardens below us
  Odors of orange-buds creep ;
Softly the winds from the river
  Over the balcony sweep ;
Pigeons are dreamily cooing
  On the tiled roof o'er the way ;
Pauses the little hand, sewing,
  Over the volume to stray,

Whence I read — prone there before her,
　Under the shade of the vine —
Of love, and all the sweet loving
　I deem can never be mine.
" Kiss me ! " I cry, " what is surer
　Than fate which biddeth me fly ?
Kiss me ! oh, what can be purer
　Than kisses kissing good-by ? "

Oh ! little hand in my own hand,
　Drooping and beautiful head,
Eyes lifted sad and beseeching,
　Words left forever unsaid !
Vanish, O vision too tender !
　What was not was not to be ;
Yet with what ravishing splendor
　Comes back that moment to me !

Moment when all my rich reading
　Read not those marvellous eyes ;
Moment when blindfolded wisdom
　Left untranslated those sighs ;
Moment when out of my keeping
　Fell the one jewel divine,
Out of my idle reach sweeping
　Ere my heart told me 't was mine.

Dew of a kiss ever cherished,
    Spell of a name never breathed ;
Voice that the scabbard of silence
    Now and forever hath sheathed !
Forth has my saddened thought hurried —
    Yonder, where cloisters are gray ;
Dusky-haired was the young novice
    Agéd nuns buried to-day.

OLGA.

PLANTED stem-deep in her red-gold hair,
   A rose trails over her shoulder white,
   As, softly robed and in gems bedight,
She sits the fairest where all are fair,
With wondrous eyes that seem everywhere
Save turned to the stage and the players there.

Those eyes, to me. are the strangest things!
   Night-blue : no, amber; no, they are green
   As cool sea-deeps in a sunflash seen.
And what a subtile, sweet perfume clings
To her garments when she stirs, and flings
About her invisible curtainings !

There, in the box with the gilded door —
   The first proscenium-box at the right —
   The prettiest woman by far in sight!
Her great, calm eyes roam the boxes o'er,
Roam, and return, and wander once more,
While forty musicians are playing " the score."

One arm on the velvet rail she leans,
    And that slow smile to her lip which comes
    Could make a halo for martyrdoms.
Who can say what its mystery means?
Ah, well, at the play there are scenes and scenes,
And a curtain which nothing tangible screens!

Her perfect face not a face salutes
    Of all the multitude turned unto her;
    And men admire, and women demur,
And this the homage of that refutes,
While grumble the drums and whistle the flutes
In the "Hunters' Chorus" of *Der Freyschütz*.

Over her shoulder the red rose trails,
    Rises and falls in the opaline light
    Of lamps that seem only burnt to-night
For that red rose and the perfume veils,
And the cheek that neither reddens nor pales
Though a thousand eyes its beauty assails.

There's that about her to make one weep,
    All perfect and peerless though she seems,
    As some one seen in those sweet, strange dreams
That come to a shining summer night's deep,
Unbroken, and yet half-conscious sleep,
When through other planets we seem to sweep.

The players play, and the great house cheers ;
   That rose, it is red on its altar white,
   Like blood on the wing of an angel bright.
And why does 't seem, as the dimness clears,
That the necklace of pearls her young throat wears
Is only a necklace of frozen tears?

OLD AGE TO TIME.

HO! Warder, who sitteth at life's great gates,
    And opeth the doors of death,
Here's a health to thee in an empty heart,
    With a mortal's failing breath!

I have marched the march, and the day is done,
    Life's rusty weapons I stack;
And close to the embers I lay me down
    Of life's last bivouac.

Nay, guardian gray, with skeleton hands,
    In vain wilt thou search my years;
Of all they were worth thou hast robbed them once,
    Ambition, love, hope, and tears!

One after one have I given to thee
    Each trinket, treasure, and dower, —
The flame of desire, the satiate sigh,
    The bud and the faded flower;

With the crimson lip and the brow divine
    Of Beauty in beauty's prime,
And the laugh that leaped from a careless heart,
    The faith that made love sublime.

All passion-wreathed into thy hands was thrown
    The golden bowl of my youth ;
And thy cynic lip sipped and soured the wine
    In the sacred vase of Truth.

In the vanished valleys what now remains?
    The vintage is plucked and pressed,
The songs are hushed, and the singers are dead,
    The vintagers all at rest.

Thy sickle hath scarred all my noblest years,
    The root of my days is cleft.
Ho ! thou who holdeth so much of my life,
    I pledge thee in what is left !

To thee, who sitteth at life's great gates
    And opeth the doors of death,
Here 's to thee, to thee, in an empty heart,
    With a mortal's failing breath !

RIME.

AFTER the last night's frost
    The autumn leaves are crisper;
And from the frigid north
    There comes a wintry whisper.
Over the icy earth
    Is spread a glittering splendor;
But from its frozen heart
    No sweet thing comes, nor tender.

After the chilling frost
    Of our last cruel parting,
Out of my frozen heart
    No tender thought is starting.
Into my icy life
    Dead leaves fall crisp and crisper;
And from my future comes
    A lone and wintry whisper.

THE EQUINOX.

A CROSS the sky, by unseen pilots steered,
  The white ships speed whose sails are spun of air ;
Across the land, with whistle wild and weird,
  The gypsy wind is wandering everywhere.

From out the sable scabbard of the clouds
  The lightning leaps, and stabs the horrent sky ;
While crashing storm-guns thunder from the shrouds
  Of misty fleets, which, battling, float on high.

King Ocean sends a million white-plumed knights
  At midnight to assault the iron shore ;
With pallid lips they hear the rocky heights
  Proclaim, "Thus far, but farther, nevermore!"

At every door a stranger I descry ;
  Wet, cold, and pale, imperiously he knocks :
He is a guest whom no one may deny,
  Beneath whose tread our trembling planet rocks, —
                    THE SWART KING EQUINOX.

THE CAPTAIN'S STORY.

THE day was hot, and we sat in the tent,—
Above us a live-oak's branches bent,
And wild birds warbled their innocent loves
In the odorous depths of orange-groves.

No fold in the flag at the door was stirred:
It hung in the heat like some bright, dead bird,
And the air was so still you could hear the tramp
Of the pacing sentry all over the camp.

It seems, sometimes, that I yet can hear
The cardinal-bird whistle loud and clear,
And the shrill, brief note of the nonpareil,
From behind the gum-tree's mossy veil,

And the startling buzz of the dragon-flies,
And the bold cicada's sudden cries,
And the rush by some sinuous serpent made,
'Neath the rank palmetto's jagged shade.

THE CAPTAIN'S STORY.

While the palpitant lizard climbs the seams
Of our shining tent in the hot sunbeams,
And the jest and laugh go from mouth to mouth
In our idle camp there away down South.

'T was our Colonel's tent, and some of us boys
    Were playing that day at euchre ;
With a deal of good-natured soldierly noise,
    Winning or losing our lucre.

The Colonel looked on ; he never played,
    But sometimes beguiled an hour
By watching the cut of heart or spade,
    Or sudden turn of a " bower."

About this man a mystery hung ;
    His history's hidden links
Were as hard to read as riddles that sprung
    Of old from the Theban sphinx.

Reserved and cold he was called by some,
    Though ever the warm abettor
Of right ; but he ne'er named friends or home,
    And never received a letter.

At the first call of our startled land
    He joined us Illinois Yanks,
And rose to his present high command
    Out of the heart of the ranks.

A braver rider ne'er held a rein,
  A bolder ne'er wore a spur :
Yet, for a comrade wrung with pain,
  No touch could be tenderer.

His hand was soft as a gentle girl's,
  His smile had a rare, sweet grace,
And a shining mass of soft black curls
  Framed in his pale dark face.

And straight he was as an Indian's arrow,
  And lithe as an Indian's bow ;
And not a thought of his soul was narrow
  For either a friend or a foe.

E'er first and foremost in the fight
  His tall form rose afar,
Like one transfigured by the might
  And majesty of war !

His brave, black eyes like scimitars
  I 've seen flash out in battle,
And blaze like God-ignited stars,
  Amid the roar and rattle

Of falling shot and bursting shell,
  The war-cloud's leaden rain,
And all the mimicry of hell
  That paints the battle-plain.

But, though he farthest rode of all,
  And dared what few would dare.
He passed unscathed by blade, or ball,
  Or shot, or shell, or snare,

As though he bore a charmèd life,
  This man who claimed no tie.
No friend, no sweetheart, child or wife,
  To mourn him should he die.

Well-educated, brave, well-bred,
  Handsome, high-toned, and young,
Speaking four languages, 't was said,
  Besides his mother-tongue, —

This our Colonel, Gustave Dupré,
  So nonchalantly bent
Above our game of cards that day,
  Within his sentried tent;

When on the sod we heard a foot
  Crush down the verdure vernal, —
A corporal with brief salute
  Said, " Some one to see you, Colonel."

We all looked up, paused in our game ;
There in the tent door's peakèd frame
A dusky woman, straight and tall,
Stood smiling down upon us all.

H

She was a stranger; whence she came
None of us knew, none knew her name;
But age and weakness, sex and port,
Appealed to every soldier's heart.

" Come in, auntie," our Colonel said,
" The sun beats hot upon your head.
Here is a seat. — No, boys; don't go, —
Be sure her mission all may know."

We boys sat where our game had stopped,
Our cards upon the table dropped;
Indifferent, careless, yet intent
Upon the stranger in the tent.

Erect, and with attentive glance,
Half question and half nonchalance,
With folded arms across his breast,
The Colonel stood beside his guest.

She took the seat, and straightened down
The folds in her blue cotton gown,
And rearranged, with wrinkled hands,
Her gingham turban's brilliant bands;

Then felt the pins, with nervous quest,
That held the kerchief across her breast,
And drew her tired feet, soiled and bare,
From sight beneath the low camp-chair.

Her faded face was swart, not black,
And marred by many a trouble-track.
For Care, the toiler, o'er her brow
Had driven a sharp, incisive plough,
Whose cruel furrows, deep and murk,
Told he 'd not idled at his work.

Within her cheeks twin hollows lay,
Wrecks of a beauty passed away.
The ruined dimple, the stranded blush,
Wont in its savage youth to rush
From cheek to brow, unchecked, untamed,
Unclouded, joyous, and unshamed,
Now lay there dead, forgot, unnamed ;
Whilst ashen tints of grief and gloom,
With which Time paints out all the bloom,
All brightness, freshness, youth, and grace,
At last from every woman's face,
Lay, sombring aught that had been fair
Of rounded grace or color there.
Yet in her dark and liquid eye
Shone out that solemn depth of power
To suffer dumbly, patiently,
Which is a woman's special dower.
This majesty of self subdued,
The lowly creature's brow imbued
With something of a Christian grace
That had become a lovelier face.
She spoke, with glance and mien abject,
And in the common dialect

That marked the plain plantation "hands,"
Well known in cane and cotton lands.
Rude were her words, but sweet her tone,
As any high-born dame would own,
And oft some quaint old Creole phrase,
Or gentle speech of gentler days,
The curious listener could detect
Mixed with her negro dialect.

"Scuse me, Cunnel, I troubles you, shore,
But, dear young massa, Ise ole and pore;
My heart was happy once, but 't appears
T' hold nuffin now but a few salt tears.
A little more toil up life's rough road,
Den dese ole shoulders 'll drop dere load.

"Ise come, as it 's been my habit to come
Wherever Ise heerd a Yankee drum,
To ax if to your knowledge dere 's been,
Froo out de ranks of de Lincum men,
A boy of mine.   He went to de Norf
When my ole massa, bress us, was worf
Sich heaps of lan' an' cane an' money,
As neber, I specs, you dreamed of, honey.
Dis boy of mine, he was strong an' peart,
An 't 'peared to me he could n't be sceart
By eber a look, or a word, or a sound:
Not even de bay of de fierce bloodhound.

THE CAPTAIN'S STORY.

Mars' Cunnel, I missed dat boy of mine
Froo de moonlight nights an' de hot sunshine,
An' my heart was neber dat weighted down
It could n't take him dar all my own,
An' feel dar was food an' light an' rest
In holdin' dat little one close to my breast."

She paused, and wiped with homely grace
The hot tears from her troubled face.

Said the Colonel, " When did he go away?"
She answered, " I can't now 'zactly say, —
Dat is, jes de year, *mo pas connais;*
But, near as I now kin recolleck,
He 'd jes about turned seven, I 'speck.
I could n't read, an' he could n't write,
An' Ise laid awake a many a night
A prayin' an' prayin' unto de Lord
Dat chile of mine would on'y sen' word
Where he was gone to, or where he was gwine;
But, bress you, dar neber cum word nor line;
An' eber sence dis yere war broke out,
It 's seemed to me, if I tried, I mought
Diskiver a clue to dat chile of mine
From some one 'noder from 'cross de line.
Kase, brave as he was, when de war begun
'T was in him to jine it de fustest one.
'So Ise sarched an' sarched under ebery rag
Dat Ise seen afloat of de Lincum flag,

A hopin' an' hopin' dese pore ole eyes
Mought see him jes once afore dey dies,
Dat dese ole arms mought hold him yet,
Afore de comin' of life's sunset,
An' my heart keeps longin' to find his lub,
Just as de wild beast longs for her cub."

"Why did he leave you?" the Colonel said,
"Sold, lost, or run away instead?"

The old mulattress dropped her face,
With the humble air of her humbled race.
"Sold? no! lost? no, nor run'd away. —
'Deed, sah! he neber dun went astray
Out of his own free will an' accord,
Nor evil-mindedness, bress de Lord!
No, no, Mars' Cunnel, my boy was good,
I wants dat ar well understood;
His heart was noble, — he loved me true,
An' many 's de time, 'twixt me an' you,
I knows he 's longed for dese lovin' arms
Dat sheltered him once from dis world's harms;
But, you see, Mars' Cunnel, 't was n't all right.
My boy was handsome, an' smart, an' — white!

"Massa was rich, dere was pride in my heart, —
I begged my boy mought be given a start,
An' not be hand an' foot tied down,
A white-skinned slave to a white man's frown.

I was younger den, an' purty, dey say ;
Well, anyhow, I had my own way,
An' de boy was sent from de ole plantation
Somewhere up Norf for an edication.

" For days arter dat I moped roun' de place,
An' cried if a chile looked up in my face ;
An' I sot on de banks of de old bayou.
A mournin' an' mournin' de long nights froo ;
For I could n't somehow set my heart to rights,
An' it an' me had some awful fights.

" I could n't help wishin' my young one back,
For a mother 's a mother, sah, white or black ;
But I had my work, an' a busy hand
'Twixt a troubled heart an' its grief will stand ;
An' I learned to say, ' It 's all for de best ;
He 'll come back some day, de Lord be blessed.'

" But year arter year came de cotton an' de cane,
But dat boy of mine cum'd neber again !
Den ole massa died, an' I was alone,
An' into de hands of strangers thrown,
An', somehow, I lost, when dey laid massa low,
Ebery trace of dat chile I longed for so !

" Den at las' cum de signs of dis yere war,
An' you Lincum soldiers here, where you are ;
An' I was sot free, an' I made up my mind
Dat, livin' or dyin', my boy I 'd find ;

An' I 'spect Ise done walked a hunnerd mile,
Barefooted, a tryin' to fine dat chile !
Now, Cunnel, dat's why I ask your consent
To jes look along froo your regiment,
An' see if 'mongst your men I can't fine
Dat growed-up pickaninny of mine."

The Colonel had heard her rambling talk,
Leaving his place now and then to walk,
As was his wont, up and down the tent,
With folded arms and brow down-bent.
Now, as she paused to dry a tear,
" Good woman," he said. " no such man here,
If I know aught of my regiment ;
But look for yourself, you have my consent."

" I wants to look for myself," she said ;
" I neber shall believe dat boy is dead
Till my poor body has toted my soul
Out of de reach of dis world's control."

" Nay. nay ! with you let us hope not dead,"
With kindly gesture, the Colonel said ;
" But think for a moment what time has done
In the changing years to change your son.
Just think what a man he now must be,
How stalwart and bearded ; it seems to me
The changes that surely have taken place
Would leave him a stranger before your face."

" Not know my chile ! " the negress said,
For the first time lifting her lowly head ;
" Not know my boy, wheresomeber he be,
If good or wicked, or bond or free?
Not know dat boy, de son dat I bore?
Oh, Mars' Cunnel, you 's jestin' shore !
Why, de stars will drop, an' de moon be spiled,
When a mother 's done forgot her child !
If my boy 's livin' he 's twenty-nine,
An' straight as de Lou'siana pine ;
An' he ain't got much of my cusséd race
Writ out, thank God ! on his brave young face.
Then he has marks ! " she said, looking up :
" His ear was bit by a terrier pup,
An' de leastest piece of it tore away,
An' I knows he carries dat mark to-day !
Den a sailor man, from some furrin land,
Pricked on the back of my boy's right hand,
In right smart style, two letters blue,
And said dey 'd allus be good as new.
De letters stood for his name, you see,
An' he told me to 'member 'em, G and D."

Suddenly pale our Colonel stood,
As if some horror had bleached his blood,
Whilst every one of us seemed to feel
His own breast pierced with red-hot steel ;
For there, on our Colonel's slim right hand,
Bright and clear was the livid brand, —

Bright and clear for us all to see,
The fatal characters, G and D !

Then came the dawn of a wild surprise
Into the woman's dilated eyes.
A swift change over her features swept,
A sudden flush to her forehead leapt. —
And then, great God! shall I e'er forget?
One hand on the Colonel's epaulette,
Whilst with the other the clustering hair
She quickly pushed from the small left ear,
And there in the delicate flesh was seen
The mark where the terrier's teeth had been.

Burst from her lips one appalling shriek !
She glared at the Colonel, but did not speak.
Just like a tigress we'd seen her spring
Up at his breast ; now, a drooping thing,
Haggard and helpless, we saw her cling
To the shuddering form she seemed to sting,
By the slight touch of her dark hand there,
Into a figure of mute despair.

Like some one suddenly stricken dumb,
With heart and veins and pulses numb,
All life, all sense a frozen flood.
For one brief space our Colonel stood ;
But now the strength came back to his grasp ;
He caught her throat in a cruel clasp ;

The tender pity that lately shed
Its gentle light on his face had fled,
And a stern white horror lay there instead.

"Unhand me, woman!" he cried, in tones
Less like words than torturing groans;
"You lie! oh, fiend! this is false as hell!
Take back the lie you have dared to tell
In this damned part you have played so well;
Take it back, — I'll throttle you else, — I say!"
She only answered, "Gustave Dupré!"

From side to side I saw him swerve,
As if each syllable struck a nerve.
Down from her throat his white hand sunk;
He reeled like one death-struck or drunk.
Upon his forehead's pallid hue
Drops of agony stood like dew.
With sudden frenzy and reckless touch
He tore himself from the woman's clutch,
And then again, with stern command,
He hoarsely bade her beside him stand.
"You gentlemen," he said, "have heard
This woman's words, nor stood aloof
Whilst she arrayed each damning proof
Of her strange claim. My soul is stirred
To madness. What have ye believed?
I burn to know myself deceived, —
To wake, shake off this fearful dream,
This horrid plot, this hellish scheme.

I cannot judge, — I cannot think, —
I totter on the awful brink
Of horrors that accumulate
Around this dark, undreamed-of fate.
Judge ye for me; though I do swear,
For yonder woman standing there
No heart-throb, instinct, new-born ties
Of kindred feeling, in me rise
Responsive to this loathsome claim
That fain would link me to her shame!
Look at us both, — here as we stand;
Forget this mark, this odious brand!
For God's sake, men, breathe out no lie,
Withhold no truth, nor aught deny. —
Say, if in cheek, or lip, or brow,
Here as we stand before you now,
A single trait alike you see
Betwixt this woman here and me.
Nay, shrink not, flinch not, nor delay;
I do command! do you obey!"

What need to stammer out replies?
He read our answers in our eyes.
Unlike, yet like, there stood the two,
Resemblance growing on our view.
As, both dismayed and both undone,
They stood, life's golden glow all gone,
Together, and yet so alone,
The stricken mother and her son.

He spoke : his voice fell cold and clear
Upon each strained, attentive ear.
" Soldiers. enough ! In every face
I read conviction of disgrace.
Are ye my friends? Then each must know
The cruel blight of this foul blow.
Are ye my foes? Then each and all
Have in the horror of my fall
Their vengeance found, their triumph won,
To see me here disgraced, undone,
Polluted, shamed. a thing to shun,
A negro mother's bastard son !

" Here, with my hand upon my sword,
I give you my untarnished word.
I knew naught of my birth or name
That shadowed me with taint or shame.
I swear this, and my word is white,
Thank God ! however in your sight
Polluted be the blood that chains
My soul to these degraded veins.
I had ambition, health, and youth,
But no suspicion of the truth.
The mystery that about me hung
No one unravelled, and I clung
To it in idle hours perchance,
And dreamed some tender, bright romance
In coming time might be unrolled.
With my name midst its honors scrolled.

Therefore I vowed to make that name
One that the noblest blood might claim
To write upon the blazoned page
Of an unsullied heritage.
From some unknown. mysterious hand
Gold flowed to aid each aim I planned ;
How hard I toiled. and what I won,
It boots not now to any one."

Then spake the woman. o'er whose face
Conflicting thoughts had seemed to chase,
As oft, in summer. on the plain,
Shadows chase shadows o'er the grain.
Her eyes, from which the tears had gushed
When first conviction o'er her rushed,
Now glittered steady. bright. and dry,
Though wet was every soldier's eye.
Upon her dusky cheeks a spot
Of glowing red burned fierce and hot,
While on her lips. firm, cold, compressed,
A subtle meaning stood confessed.

" Massa," she said, and every word
Burned to the brain of him who heard, —
" Mars' Cunnel, Ise gwine to go away.
I don't want you to rue de day
When fust I cum yer, a pore ole tramp,
Disturbin' de peace of dis yer camp.
Somehow or 'noder Ise made a mistake ;
Folks will sometimes when de heart's fit to break.

'Scuse me, — Ise giv' you a heap of bother;
Ole people 's stupid somehow or 'nother.
But, Mars' Cunnel, and ebery one,
Better folks dan me dis war 's undone,
An' whar I cum from dey tink it 's dazed
My pore ole brain, and dey say Ise crazed.

" Ise gwine away right now, — Ise tired, —
It is n't much to which Ise 'spired :
I jes thought if I could fine my boy
Den life would shet wid a sudden joy.
Ise pleased myself for many a year
Tinkin' how, as a man, dat boy 'd appear ;
An' many a pang has my heart forsook
When I thought jes how de chile mus' look, —
How tall he 'd growed, and how pleased he 'd be
When I foun' him out, an' he know'd 't was me !
But, Mars' Cunnel, it 's plain an' clear
If I sarched foreber he 'd not be here :
I don't see any but what would be
Ten tousand times too good for me. —
So smart an' peart, brave an' upright,
An' honored too, an' all so white !
Ise gwine on huntin' dat boy of mine,
Froo de moonlight nights an' de hot sunshine,
A rockin' my grief by de ole bayou,
And nussin' de dream dat neber comes true,
Dat yet I 'll fine him once agen
In de God-blest ranks of de Lincum men.

Whar de gray moss swings on de pecan-tree
Dere 's a cabin yet, an' a place for me
To rest in, when, a tired ole rover,
I knows dat de hunt for dat chile is over.
Jes for a minute, — ah, mon Dieu !
Cunnel — your face, — but 't was n't true !
No. — not wid de proud, an' great, an' brave
Could rank de son of de pore ole slave.

"Massa, Ise gwine, — Ise slow to go, —
But den Ise ole an' tired, you know ;
Don't mine dese tears dat my face has wet,
A mother 's a mother, an' can't forget,
Though her skin be brack as de day unborn,
De baby dat once on her heart was worn.
Cunnel, good-by.   Oh, let my lips
Lay jes once 'gin your finger-tips,
Jes one kiss dar, — one, soft and sly,
Unknownst to any one — good-by !
Ise gwine right now, — of course you see,
Your hand — dose letters was nuflin to me.
My boy's — name — was n't —   Oh, my God !"
Gasping, smiling, down to the sod,
At the very feet of our Colonel brave,
Slowly sank down the poor old slave.

Strong with a strength we had failed to know,
Felled where none of us felt a blow,
Great in that grand, unselfish pride
Which heroes and martyrs hath glorified,

Prone she sank at our Colonel's side :
And, as she fell, her fading eyes
Turned with one yearning, pleading gaze,
Mingled yet with a glad surprise,
Up to the Colonel's haggard face ;
Then fell away with that mute endeavor
The dying make to give up forever
All that they hold of dearest worth,
Or sacred value upon the earth,
And turned to us, as in the tent,
Saddened and shocked, we o'er her bent,
And, searching our faces one by one,
Whispered, " Your Cunnel is not my son ! "
With these brief words, all glorified
Her features grew, — once, twice, she sighed,
Lifted her hands, and spread them o'er
Her dusky face, and spoke no more.
" Send for the surgeon ! " the Colonel said ;
On his own knee he pillowed her head.

The surgeon came.   On the swarthy breast
Slightly his practised hand he pressed ;
Then, with a shake of his sturdy head,
" Boys," he muttered, " this woman is dead !
Send for a stretcher, — how came she here ?
Anything now must serve for a bier.
There 's news afloat : the enemy lie
Strongly entrenched, it is said, hard by ;
But of course you know it ; there 's work ahead :
Better make haste and bury your dead."

Then with a laugh, and a soldier's jest,
Unaware of what sore oppressed
Every heart that around him beat,
He turned away with hurrying feet ;
Calling back, as he passed from sight,
" Hot work for us all before midnight."

 . . . . .

Responsive to the careless word
So lightly said, so keenly heard,
Swept through our veins that martial fire
Which every soldier doth inspire.
We half forgot what late had been
In picturing the coming scene ;
And each man's hand was on his sword,
And each man's foot turned toward the door,
When one imploring, earnest word
Caused every one to halt once more.

The Colonel stood beside the dead,
His own cloak o'er the form was spread,
And o'er his head seemed to have passed
Years since we looked upon him last.

" My men ! " he said, " this doomèd hand
Bears, in its blue and livid brand,
The vile insignia of disgrace
That marked my mother's lowly race.
Nay ! do not take its cruel stain
Within your honest grasp again !

You will? then let it e'en be so."
And as we gave him one by one
The clasp he would but could not shun,
There came a soft and tender glow
Across the pallor of his cheek,
Which spoke, as never words could speak,
How precious unto him had been
The good-will of his fellow-men.

"Great God! a father does his worst
Who leaves his son a blood accursed!"
At last he said; "ah, worse than chains
The burden of defiled veins!
But of this thing enough. We hear
Impending battle drawing near.
You know, ere now, what fights I 've shared,
You know what dangers I have dared,
You know if e'er a craven led
Where comrades fell and comrades bled.
You know, if e'er where foes were met,
This hand or sabre faltered yet!
Remembering this, if for this fight
I do renounce all rank or right. —
You will forgive? You will not blame
Nor whisper *coward* with my name?
Soldiers! I cannot forth again, —
What good fate held for me has been;
My star has sunk, my day is sped.
I will not follow where I led!
Nor will I meet the signs of scorn

Sure in some comrade to be born,
Who looks for honor or disgrace
Only in records of one's race.
These smitten hands resign all claim
To future glory, future fame.
Where is the lip to name the good
Found in a white man's negro blood?
Here, with this last grasp of my hand,
I yield forever my command.
Forth to the fight, and fare ye well!
My future, be it heaven or hell,
Can make, can mar, not yours — adieu!
Unto your country be ye true!"
With these last words, a gleam of steel
Met our stark eyes, — we saw him reel, —
Toward him rushed his aim to thwart.
Too late! his own sword kissed his heart;
And pale and dead before us lay
Our gallant Colonel — Gustave Dupré.

1874.

THE BATHER.

WARM from her waist her girdle she unwound,
    And cast it down on the insensate turf;
Then copse, and cove, and deep-secluded vale
She scrutinized with keen though timid eyes,
And stood with ear intent to catch each stir
Of leaf, or twig, or bird-wing rustling there.
Her startled heart beat quicker even to hear
The wild bee woo the blossom with a hymn,
Or hidden insect break its lance of sound
Against the obdurate silence. Then she smiled,
At her own fears amused, and knew herself
God's only image by that hidden pool.
Then from its bonds her wondrous hair she loosed. —
Hair glittering like spun glass, and bright as though
Shot full of golden arrows. Down below
Her supple waist the soft and shimmering coils
Rolled in their bright abundance, goldener
Than was the golden wonder Jason sought.

Her fair hands then, like white doves in a net,
A moment fluttered mid the shining threads,
As with a dexterous touch she higher laid

The gleaming tresses on her shapely head,
Beyond the reach of rudely amorous waves.
Then from her throat her light robe she unclasped,
And dropped it downward, with a blush that rose
The higher as the garment lower fell.

Then cast she off the sandals from her feet,
And paused upon the brink of that blue lake,—
A sight too fair for either gods or men,
An Eve untempted in her Paradise.

The waters into which her young eyes looked
Gave back her image with so true a truth,
She blushed to look, but blushing looked again ;
As maidens to their mirrors oft return
With bashful boldness once again to gaze
Upon the crystal page that renders back
Themselves unto themselves, until their eyes
Confess their love for their own loveliness.
Her rounded cheeks, in each of which had grown,
With sudden blossoming, a fresh red rose,
She hid an instant in her dimpled hands ;
Then met her pink palms up above her head.
And whelmed her white shape in the welcoming wave.

Around each lithesome limb the waters twined,
And with their lucent raiment robed her form ;
And as her hesitating bosom sunk
To the caresses of bewildered waves,
They foamy pearls from their own foreheads gave

For her fair brow, and showered in her hair
The evanescent diamonds of the deep.

Thus dallying with the circumfluent tide,
Her loveliness half hidden, half revealed,
An Undine with a soul, she plunged and rose ;
Whilst the white graces of her rounded arms
She braided with the blue of wandering waves,
And saw the shoulders of the billows yield
Before the even strokes of her small hands,
And laughed to see, and held her crimson mouth
Above the crest of each advancing surge,
Like a red blossom pendent o'er a pool,—
Till, done with the invigorating play,
Once more she gained the bank, and once again
Saw her twin image in the waters born.

From the translucent wave each beauty grew
To strange perfection.   Never statue, wrought
By cunning art to fulness of all grace,
And kissed to life by love, could fairer seem
Than she who stood upon that grassy slope
So fresh, so human, so immaculate !
Out from the dusky cloisters of the wood
The nun-like winds stole with a saintly step,
And dried the bright drops from her panting form,
As she with hurried hands once more let down
The golden drapery of her glorious hair,
That fell about her like some royal cloak
Dropped from the sunset's rare and radiant loom.

GOLD.

I.

Gold, virgin gold !
Secret scrolled on the ages old ;
Swift eye-light of the Infinite,
Searching earth, that palace of Time,
With penetrant rays of its glance sublime ;
  Yellow blood
  Of solitude,
Left concealed where it congealed
When God declared the round world " good" :
  Pangs of birth
  The infant earth
Knew when hurled, a perfect world,
  To its place
In the welcoming arms of space ;
  Creation's glees
  And jubilees,
Transmuted by the first sunrise
Into precious alchemies ;
  Gleams chaotic
  Of laws despotic,
As yet unripped from the world's dark crypt ;

Cipher of silence, graven deep
Where darkness and where danger sleep;
    Magic ring
    Of marrying,
That gave to Time a bride sublime;
    Primal kiss
    Of Genesis,
    Thrilling through
    The unfathomed New.
Poem of the pristine ages
Penned on the Beginning's pages;
Grand epithalamium sung
When the World and Time were young;
    Harmonies of centuries
    Tangled with eternities;
    Unsoiled, unsoiling,
    Unreviled and unreviling,
    Broad-sown, unknown,
    Unbought, unsold,
      Gold, virgin gold!

      II.

    Gold, beaten gold!
Hunted from its secret shrines
In the dungeons of the mines;
    Stained with human strife,
    Gained with human life,
    Black with falsehood's grime,
    Red with smirch of crime;

Torn from Nature's savage shoulders,
From her gulches, from her bowlders,
While the nations stood and heard her
Voices crying, " Wrong." and " Murder,"
" Woe," and " Sorrow," " Pain." and " Terror,"
And the echoes echoed. " Error : "
Stretched beneath the clank and clamor
Of the oscillating hammer.
        Which a glamour spreads,
    While it swings, while it rings,
    That the multitude brings
        To see who weds
            Gold, virgin gold,
To the whims of that tyrant old. —
        The world, which laughs and frets,
    Remembers. forgets,
        Loves. and denies,
            Yet hugs its prize, —
Gold, talismanic gold !
            See it quiver !
            See it shiver !
See the bright, crepuscular foil
Stretch, and shudder, and recoil ;
See it tremble, see it strive ;
See it writhing, see it breathing, —
            'T is alive !
        Coiling. twisting,
        Vainly resisting
        The quickened blows
        That smite its throes.

'T is a slave :
Mute and brave,
Still a slave.
Red gold, dead gold.
Twisted, graven, knotted, scrolled ;
Woven into Beauty's hair :
Diademing scowling Care,
And his tired brother Toil, —
Care and Toil, twin kings
Of the kingdom called Turmoil.
Smitten gold,
Written gold!
Mystic signet, aureate
On the outstretched hand of Fate,
Its triumphant glitter blent
With Occident and Orient ;
Scintillant its lurid gleam
Where the Hindoo maidens dream ;
Radiant where Memnon waits
The opening of Ra's splendid gates,
Where the long Nile's amber waters
Mirror Afric's dusky daughters ;
Symbol of a law austere,
Stamped on sphere and hemisphere ;
Circled into wedding rings, —
Those mysterious, fateful things, —
Throning Vice in Virtue's palace,
Moulded into priestly chalice,
Yellow gold,
Mellow gold,

Beaten, burnished, rended, rolled ;
Glimmering. shimmering,
Offering laid at every shrine,
Bed for gems from every mine ;
Fettering the ivory-wristed,
With the robes of wantons twisted,
By the purest hand caressed,
Gleaming on the vilest breast.
Blent with sorrow. blent with mirth,
Veiling death and crowning birth.
Woven into gain and loss,
Fashioned into crown and cross, —
Decorator, desolator.
Gold, beaten gold !

III.

Gold, coinéd gold !
Molten, measured, stamped, and sold ;
Fatal spell
Hurled up from hell.
Or down to mortals from Heaven's portals ;
Blessing, evil.
Angel, devil. —
Sin and shame defied for it,
Hope and love denied for it ;
Pleasure's double,
Twin of trouble,
With its fatal serpent eyes
Entering earth's Paradise,

Controlling fate of Church and State,
Which from the Grandé to the Ganges
Rings its multitudinous changes.
    All sing the king
      Who, Janus-featured,
      Double-natured,
As a blessing, as a curse,
For the better, for the worse,
Sits throned above a universe
Which, at his smile or at his frown,
Elate arises or bows down.
      Swiftly smiting,
      Swift delighting,
    Yellow Demon, smirking Leman ;
Heart of virtue, soul of sin,
Of Right and Wrong the equal twin ;
      Vile deceiver,
      Sweet reliever,
To the worthless lending worth ;
      Joy revealing,
      Gladness stealing.
With its bounty, with its dole,
Ruling body, ruling soul ;
Sounding ocean's deepest deeps,
Soaring where the lightning sleeps ;
Delving in the dreariest mines,
Kneeling at the happiest shrines ;
Aiding eager-handed science
Triumphantly to bid defiance
    To the powers of earth and air,

Air and water, earth and fire ;
   Sending Learning from his throne
To girdle earth from zone to zone,
To sound the seas, to scale the skies,
To rend from stars their mysteries.
And bound the world with enterprise ;
At the funeral. at the feast.
Mightiest oft where seeming least,
     Type of error,
     Type of terror,
   Tyrant of the day and hour
   Magic and mysterious Power ;
     Life's enjoyment,
     Joy's alloyment ;
      Yellow, ~~mare~~, *Snare*
     Foul and fair ;
From the cradle to the grave
Making man its veriest slave, —
    Oh the want of it !
    Oh the vaunt of it !
    Gold. coinéd gold !

FROM YEAR TO YEAR.

THIS is the sofa, and that is the chair,
And the English ivy is twining there
    The marble Dante's brow ;
And Raphael's Mary is looking down
At Murillo's monk with the cowlèd crown,
    The same as a year ago.

The same? No : nothing is ever the same
From year to year, that the tongue can name :
    This scene is not, I know. —
For there by that curtain of dainty lace,
At the balconied window, I miss a face
    That was there a year ago.

I looked on it from the ottoman there,
And it looked at me from that velvet chair,
    A girl's face pure as snow.
She looked like a being divinely bright,
'Twixt the Holy Mother and monk, that night, —
    That night just a year ago.

The south wind breathed in the curtain of lace,
And the marble Dante gazed in her face, —
    Her face pale as his own ;
While my heart, like a bird all plumed for flight,
Stood poised on the wings of a hope that night,
    Then soared to heights unknown.

Ah me ! I remember the rush and the thrill
Of that flight of my heart, when stars stood still
    Compared to its wild career !
Ah me ! I remember it seemed so strange
To believe that time had the power to change
    All things from year to year.

The flowers in this slender Etruscan vase,
With the emerald cup and the silver base,
    Are Medellin roses rare ;
I smelt them that night when I knelt at her feet ;
They were deathly white, they were deathly sweet,
    On her brow and her braided hair.

I could smite the vase for its scented flowers,
I could hate this room for its vanished hours ;
    I could curse the painted stare
Of the cruel monk, the Madonna mild,
Who saw that night how cruelly smiled
    The girl in the velvet chair !

Ah, maiden woman ! I believe even now
That hour is shading your perfect brow,
  The matchless curve of your lip ;
And Medellin roses make you turn white :
Their odor is strong, and out of their sight
  Your troubled eyes love to slip.

Yes. this is the sofa, and that is the chair,
And the English ivy is twining there,
  Where the books and the marbles lie ;
And the painted Madonna hangs in her frame,
And seems unchanged, but she is not the same —
  Any more than are you and I.

THE GRANDMOTHER'S PRAYER.

THEY laid the young child on the grandmother's knee,—
  A beautiful boy, immortality's heir ;
His brow a pure page from life's handwriting free,
  His heart yet untroubled by sorrow or care.
The grandmother bent o'er the fair little form,
  And smiled a sweet welcome, caressing and warm ;
Then, laying her hand on the innocent head,
  " Oh, bless it and save it ! " she tenderly said.

The tocsin of battle was heard far and wide ;
  The young soldier knelt at his grandmother's knee,
And, lifting his brow to her fond kiss of pride,
  Said, " Grandmother, hast thou no blessing for me ? "
She bent her kind face, now well stricken in years,
  And like a new baptism fast fell her tears,
As, clasping her hands o'er the manly young head,
  " Oh, bless him and save him ! " she fervently plead.

The combat was over; the wounded and slain
Lay gory and grim where their spirits had sped;
The whispering winds that stole over the plain
Grew dumb in the horrible hush of the dead.
There, fair in his slumber as brave in his life,
The soldier youth lay mid the wrecks of the strife;
His lip, which the battle had robbed of its breath,
Still smiled as it froze 'neath the finger of Death.

Woe-mantled, the living came seeking him there;
They bore the young form to the grandmother's side.
Her wrinkled hands smoothed out the battle-tossed hair,
And she kissed the brave lips which smiling had died.
Again the swift tears from her aged eyes fell
O'er the darling her old heart had cherished so well;
Then, kneeling to pray for the young spirit sped,
" Oh, bless it and save it ! " she solemnly said.

" Bless it and save it ! " — Oh, eloquent prayer,
How joyeth the heart in its beautiful light !
So brief, comprehensive, its little words bear
. A meaning which compasseth all in His sight.
To be saved from the billows and breakers of life,
To be blessed amid worldly temptations and strife;
To be saved when all this that is earthly is o'er;
To be blessed, to be saved, — what heart could ask more?

LIFE'S MUTATIONS.

"AYE!" croaks the crooked crone,
        As she walks the forest through,
"Flaunt your roses, maiden,
    And flash your eyes of blue!
For life goes round in circles, —
    As I am, you may be ;
The tender bud and the crispen leaf
    Grow on the self-same tree!"

"Girl, bless your bridal wreath,"
    Saith the corpse upon its bier, —
"Orange-flowers and beauty
    Must all at last end here!
For life goes round in circles, —
    Where I am, you must lie ;
On the self-same stem where roses bloom,
    There do the roses die!"

" Toss not your pence so rudely,"
    To the prince the pauper cried;
" Fortune, fickle coquette,
    Not always favors pride.
For life goes round in circles,
    It swirleth up and down ;
To-day, who plays the Jester may
    To-morrow wear the crown ! "

" Walk not so calm and stately,"
    Righteousness whispered to Crime ;
" Temptation brings strange victims
    At last to the rack of Time !
For life goes round in circles ;
    Where I am, you may be ;
The good ship sails, and the good ship sinks,
    All on the self-same sea ! "

AT THE WHEEL.

T HAT "constant employment is constant enjoyment,"
      I often have heard the dear old people say ;
But fuller the measure of my simple pleasure
    If Robin and I were but roaming to-day.

Here I must keep busy, though weary and dizzy,
    Still whirling my wheel, and still spinning my thread ;
Though harvests are yellow, and bird-notes are mellow,
    And lips of wild roses glow fervently red !

The path through the meadow lies cool in the shadow,
    The mischievous brook laughs aloud in the vale ;
The cry of the plover floats tunefully over
    The rattle of osiers that redden the swale.

The bee, from the bosom of red-clover blossom,
    Has hurried to sip of the buckwheat in bloom ;
The blush of the thistle, the blackbird's clear whistle,
    Are blent with the summer-day's light and perfume.

The soft wandering gale fills a silvery sail
  That idly floats by on yon far-away stream,
And a frail spirit-boat 'neath the other doth float,
  Faintly fair, like some beautiful dream of a dream.

With odors of myrtle the voice of the turtle
  Comes drowsily up from the valley below ;
I hear the dull rapping of woodpecker's tapping
  The bark where the hollow old sycamores grow.

The beetle is humming of autumn days coming,
  And swings in its leaf hammock hung in the vale ;
The lily gasps faintly as, passionless, saintly,
  It stands in the path of the libertine gale.

The clink, clink of the blade rises clear from the glade
  Where, sharpening the scythe, stands the whistling mower ;
While the gossiping crow, on his tall hickory bough,
  Sits moodily muttering his meaningless lore.

There are mystical fingers whose gentle touch lingers,
  It seems, as I listen, on yon golden plain,
There blending, and shading, and lovingly braiding
  The sunbeams astray with the beard of the grain.

With tired hand twirling the wheel that keeps whirling,
  The wearisome spindle I speed all the day ;
With the whirl of the wheel how my brain seems to reel,
  And longs from the dull hum to hurry away !

Oh, how gladly I'll watch the first star-ray to catch,
  That shall tell when the sun lieth low in the west;
When swallows home darting tell day is departing,
  And night brings the toiler sweet guerdon of rest.

Then over the " hollow" and green " summer fallow "
  I shall hear the loud summons of " Co' boss ! co' boss ! "
While " Lineback " and " Dover," breaths sweetened with
    clover,
  The cool, fragrant pastures come slowly across,

With " Brownie" and " Daisy," milk-laden and lazy,
  The gentle-eyed heifer half-standing aloof;
While the dew-laden grass gently yields as they pass
  To the lingering print of each slowly raised hoof.

Then away, then away, as dies the long day,
  O'er the path that leads down to the sycamore grove,
Where dear Robin will wait by the old wicket gate,
  With a smile for my eyes, and a heart for my love !

RILMA'S FAREWELL.

D EAR Love! the words are said,
   Thou know'st we may not wed;
Farewell to thee, farewell:
Upon the beach I stand
And kiss to thee my hand;
   Yonder the white sails swell!

Yea! on the beach I stand,
And to thee kiss my hand;
   My lips thou might'st not touch, —
'T were little, yet too much,
'Twixt thee and me, dear friend!
   Therefore so let it end.

Surely thou know'st the word,
The bitterest ever heard, —
   The woful whisper, "parted"?
'T is but a swift, pale breath,
And yet 't is death, 't is death
   Unto the loving-hearted!

7*

I see the widening space
'Twixt mine and thy dear face,
   I know my heart must break;
I know that thou art gone.
I know I am alone,
   Yet smile for thy dear sake.

Pale, sad, bereft of speech,
I pace the shingly beach,
   I linger on the sands,
And wring and wring my hands;
I know my aching heart
   Must go where'er thou art;

Though through my falling tears
I see a wall of years
   Dividing thee from me,
As land divides the sea;
O'er it hope cannot soar, —
   I know we meet no more!

Thou wilt go on thy way,
Sad for a year and day.
   By slowly fading embers;
A man's heart joys again,
A woman's dies of pain:
   He laughs, while she — remembers!

HOW LONG?

THE storm has put out the stars, and the night is
    blind;
But the Hours grope their way through the darkness, on to
    a time
When Morning, the pink-palmed, shall come to the door
    of the East.
And with fragrant fingers beckon one out of the gloom,
And, choosing him, kiss him with kisses that shine like
    light,
And, kissing him, call him her chosen, the Prince of the
    Dawn.

The storm has put out the stars and my life is blind.
I grope in the darkness back to the star of a night
When one star shining illumined the world for me;
One star, — it went down, and for me it rose nevermore.
Long have I waited in darkness to greet it again;
Waited for it to lay on my uplifted forehead
The white kiss of its rare and wonderful radiance;

Waited and watched for it to lead me upward,
Out of the drenching darkness and gloom of the night.
Will it come back to me never?
Does any star set forever?
How long, how long, must I wait?

IN DREAMS.

A PRESENCE felt, but never seen ;
  A voice not heard, but understood ;
A shadowy bliss that comes between
  My soul and my soul's widowhood ;

A touch upon my slumbering brow ;
  A breath upon my eyelids pressed ;
A vision fading, that but now
  In dreams my dreamy lip caressed ;

A voiceless echo, soft and sweet,
  And held in tremulous control,
That wakes my wild heart's busy beat,
  And softly serenades my soul ;

The coming of a soft eclipse, —
  Love's shadow 'twixt the world and me,
Beneath whose veil my glowing lips
  Betray my spirit's ecstasy ;

A reaching after glorious aims ;
  A searching of the soul's intents ;
A looking up from earthly shames ;
  A kneeling at new sacraments ;

The vision of a soul made great
  And grand by might of mighty needs ;
The vision of a soul elate
  And strong with strength of mighty deeds ;

A sense of something sentient
  That holds me in a spirit clasp ;
The yearning of my Being, bent
  To grasp that which eludes my grasp ;

The cool of dews upon my face,
  Dropped from the broken dusk of dawn ;
A perished joy, a vanished grace,
  A weary sigh for something gone ;

The breaking of sleep's golden thread ;
  The clashing of life's brazen rings ;
A gathering gloom, a glory fled,
  A coming back to earthly things.

IT RAINS.

A SUDDEN sweetness unto all the world
   The summer rain is bringing;
Glad odors from the lush, green meadow grass,
   Like larks, are upward springing.

The scent of blossoms, growing in a wood,
   Just now above me floated,
And from a hidden nest a thrush's song,
   Duetted and devoted.

The fainting earth, like some fresh-watered flower,
   Revives beneath its wetting,
And flings, from out a thousand fragrant nooks,
   Sweet things I was forgetting.

From cypress swamps an herby odor comes,
   Where weedy wonders waken,
To pour their grateful gladness out for drops
   Upon their petals shaken.

And roses, sighing by the wayside, lift
　　Their gentle, Juncy faces
To read the strange handwriting of the rain
　　In unfamiliar places.

The startled violets tremble, as they drop
　　Their heads to deeper hiding,
Afraid of this mere phantom of a storm,
　　Across the green earth gliding.

The sweet of all the scented shower is mine,
　　No balmy touch has missed me ;
Why has it waked the memory of dear lips
　　That one day stooped and kissed me !

UP THE HILL.

I LAY my head on a daisy bed,
  My couch is of feathery ferns ;
The sweetest bird that ever was heard
  Is singing and silent by turns.
Just at my side, with a laughing tide,
  That toys with the odorous mosses,
A mountain stream, like one in a dream,
  Impatiently turns and tosses.

O vagrant rover, rollicking brook, —
  Say, whither so fast this morning?
Hast brought to me from some forest nook
  No word of cheer nor of warning?
From every accent of Nature's tongue
  Some truth is to be translated ;
Why then are thy mountain ripples rung?
  With what is thy swift tide freighted?

You answer, low, that " yon blossom's brow
  Should show you a sign more tender ; "
And now you quaff, with mischievous laugh,
  Yon lily-cup's scarlet splendor !

I hear your fleet, meandering feet
　　Upon the jewel-like pebbles ;
Where shadows fall, or where glooms appall,
　　I hear your tunefulest trebles.

Upon your path the opulent fields
　　And woods their loveliness squander ;
You, like a young friar in disguise,
　　Among them jauntily wander.
Here, on your breast you tenderly place
　　The sweetly capricious roses ;
There, from the gentian's jealous face
　　You kiss the tear it discloses.

Upon thy brink the gay bobolink
　　Has stilled his audacious throat,
As if to hear, with a critic's ear,
　　Thy soft and musical note.
Beneath thy brim thy jubilant hymn
　　Is thrilling the silvery water
With notes of praise for the wondrous ways
　　Of Nature, thy *Alma Mater!*

O mountain singer, my mission name !
　　Say, what should my hands be doing?
Say, what is the noblest earthly aim
　　My soul should be now pursuing?

Within my grasp what good is shrined?
　　What in my life worth living?
To bless or benefit mankind,
　　What in my grasp worth giving?

Thou, newly come from thy nature-home, —
　　Its pure and unworldly preachings
Surely to-day can to me convey
　　Profound and exalted teachings.
Dost to me bear surcease from care,
　　Or somnolent potions for sorrow ;
News from my dead, or cure for the dread
　　Unfaltering steps of To-morrow?

Life's sweet days pass, and the gulf of years
　　Its vague deep opes to receive them ;
Life's sweet joys die, — into cloth of tears
　　Time's shuttles busily weave them.
Long-cherished faiths, to the soul endeared,
　　Agnostic spectres are haunting ;
From shrines that the inmost heart revered,
　　Doubt's fatal banners are flaunting.

Dost thou not bring, in the song you sing
　　With so much innocent riot,
The subtile chimes of the sweet old times,
　　Which knew not sorrow's fiat ;

Nor bring the spell, remembered well,
   Dear hands once cast around me,
When sweeter bays, when trustier praise,
   And truer friends had crowned me?

Or if thy coming unto me brings
   Themes worthier of my heeding,
Why hid'st, in whatever thy gladness sings,
   A lesson beyond my reading?
Dost bid my soul to no longer yearn
   For the heights it ne'er has gained ;
To cease to struggle, and toil, and burn
   For the Ever Unattained?

Ah ! where does it smile, that wonderful Isle,
   The Unattainable Land, —
With the dampened fires, and the broken lyres,
   That strew its untrodden strand ;
With its tired slaves, and its conquered braves,
   And its beacon of vain endeavor ;
With weird control, luring soul after soul
   To seek it forever and ever ;

With its feverish flashes, its fervid schemes,
   Its fascinations despotic,
Its dying smiles, and its beautiful dreams,
   Its aims and visions chaotic ;

With its passion-flowers, and the ruined hopes
 On its lurid beaches burning;
With the shattered lives on its fatal slopes,
 Its pilgrims sadly returning?

Hast naught to say? Then away, away!
 Go turn the mill in the meadow;
Go lure the gale, in the willowed vale,
 To chase thy shine and thy shadow.
The simple lay I have sung to-day
 By to-morrow will have perished;
Thy mystic song will to earth belong
 When mine is left uncherished!

ASHES OF ROSES.

REMEMBER thee? Dear Love! the thievish years,
Which steal so much from every human joy,
Have robbed thine image of its frame of tears,
But left it tints time never can destroy.
On Memory's golden easel here it stands,
In all the rare perfection that was thine
When first, upon Life's shining, morning sands,
Thy glad young face was lifted up to mine!

As then, my darling, here thy beauty glows, —
One white hand prisoning its pretty mate,
The dimple ambushed in thy cheek's red rose,
Thy chestnut curls, thy brow immaculate,
Thy bosom swelling with its happy sighs,
Thy life yet free from sorrow's first eclipse,
The smile that grew and budded in thine eyes,
And bloomed at last upon thy dewy lips.

Ah, fair the picture! From the world's rude strife
I turn, its sacred loveliness to kiss;
Though all the choicest roses of my life
Were ground to ashes, Love, to paint me this!

No more my heart against it breaks with sighs,
Throbs with mad passion, tastes of bitter lees ;
But there is something dims my wistful eyes,
More fond, more true, and tenderer far than these.

If but the heart a portal once unlock
For love to stand within the mystic gate,
Its footprints, like the impress on a rock,
Dead leaves may fill, but naught obliterate.
Regret may fade, woe weep itself to death,
But love so close to the supernal clings,
Though death and burial it encompasseth,
In Memory's Heaven it wears immortal wings.

Would I forget thee, that thou didst not dare
Thy life's bright girdle then to cast round me ?
Not love thee, that my selfish, passionate prayer
Linked not with mine thy fairer destiny ?
Do we love less the rose we may not take ;
Call less than star the star beyond our grasp ;
Disdain the precious dream we do but wake
To find unreal in our eager clasp ?

Nay, darling, as of old I keep thee yet,
Without one blemish on thy beauty laid,
Shrined in a niche my tears have often wet,
But whence no faithless thought has ever strayed.
Around the lonely ruins of my years
The joy of having known thee twines alway,
And flings o'er crumbling hopes and wasting fears
A radiance that deifies decay.

NOT.

—

COME to me, tears, if come to me ye must,
   In hours like these, when all the world is far;
When all the bygone brightness of my days
On my lone heart is shining like a star.
Come ye, while men remember but my smiles,
Think of my presence as a thing of songs,
Envy my lot, and, in these silent hours,
Dream of my joys in contrast to their wrongs.

Come, as the raindrops from the cloudlet come,
The burden from the cloudlet's heart to bear.
Sparkle and shine, white diamonds of a mine
Whose jewel-light the world may never share.
Thy gleam shall show me, for a little while,
The youth-coast, with its rose and amber shore
From which men gayly sail, then ever yearn
To drop life's iron anchors there once more.

I think to-night of dear, affectioned lips,
Whose kisses rest in that unlettered urn,
White in some niche of every human life,
Whence love and tenderness no more return.

Come to me, tears, my lonely spirit thrill
As gentle tropic winds thrill tropic palms ;
Fall ye, as fell those farewells which awoke
My heart forever from its summer calms.

I am alone, as is the pine alone,
Left where has fallen the surrounding wood ;
Sunshine about me, but my hidden heart
Unbrightened in its voiceless solitude.
Come to me, tears, — come like the twilight mist
That o'er the dusk and lonely valley gleams ;
Veil from me Memory's disappointing plains,
Where rise the empty tents of life's vain dreams.

8

SURRENDERED.

TO-DAY, from out my life's fair garden fell
    A fruit perfected.   On the scanty bough
Of Friendship, I can see, alas! too well,
Where once it grew, a saddening voidness now.
A goodly graft it was; one I had wound
With my own heart, to bind it safe and warm
From frosts and tempests which too oft had found
And hurt dear things I strove to shield from harm.
A human heart was faithful ligature,
But to the twig who may its bloom secure?

Ah, well! what matters it?   Ripe fruit will fall;
Perfection's twin is Progress, not Decay;
The bough that grows across the orchard wall
Must drop its apple on the outer way.
'T is true, beyond the limit of my reach
Has passed a life my own life must forego;
But it is in the world, to learn, to teach,
To gain, to give, to struggle, and to grow.
'T was mine, 't is not mine, — what should I regret?
A sun comes ever up, for one sun set.

WAYNE.

YE hills of Wayne! ye hills of Wayne!
In dreams I see your slopes again;
In dreams my childish feet explore
Your daisied dells beloved of yore;
In dreams, with eager feet, I press
Far up your heights of loveliness,
And stand, a glad-eyed girl again,
Upon the happy hills of Wayne!

I see once more the glad sunrise
Break on the world's awakening eyes;
I see once more the tender corn
Shake out its banners to the morn;
I see the sleepy valleys kissed
And robbed of all their robes of mist,
When laughing Day is queen again
Of all the verdant hills of Wayne.

I bind about my childish brow
The bloomy thorn-trees' scented snow;

I see upon the fading flowers
The fatal fingers of the hours ;
I see the distant village spire
Catch on its tip a star of fire,
As in my dreams the sun again
Goes down behind the hills of Wayne.

The cowboy's coaxing call across
The meadow comes, — "Co' boss, co' boss!"
And milky-odored cattle lift
Their hoofs among the daisy drift.
The day is over all too soon ;
And up the sky the haunted moon
Glides with its ghost, and bends again
Above the wooded hills of Wayne.

Ah! I have laughed in many a land ;
And I have sighed on many a strand
And lonely beach, where written be
The solemn scriptures of the sea ;
And I have climbed the grandest heights
The moon of midnight ever lights ;
But memory turned from all, again
To kneel upon the hills of Wayne.

Ye hills of Wayne! ye hills of Wayne!
Ye woods, ye vales, ye fields of grain !
Ye scented morns, ye blue-eyed noons !
Ye ever unforgotten moons !

No matter where my latest breath
Shall freeze beneath the kiss of death, —
May some one bear me back again
To sleep among the hills of Wayne!

A WOMAN'S WISH.

WOULD I were lying in a field of clover,
    Of clover cool and soft, and soft and sweet,
With dusky clouds in deep skies hanging over,
    And scented silence at my head and feet.

Just for one hour to slip the leash of Worry,
    In eager haste, from Thought's impatient neck,
And watch it coursing, in its heedless hurry
    Disdaining Wisdom's call or Duty's beck!

Ah! it were sweet, where clover clumps are meeting
    And daisies hiding, so to hide and rest;
No sound except my own heart's sturdy beating,
    Rocking itself to sleep within my breast, —

Just to lie there, filled with the deeper breathing
    That comes of listening to a wild bird's song!
Our souls require at times this full unsheathing, —
    All swords will rust if scabbard-kept too long;

And I am tired, — so tired of rigid duty,
  So tired of all my tired hands find to do !
I yearn, I faint, for some of life's free beauty,
  Its loose beads with no straight string running through !

Aye, laugh, if laugh you will, at my crude speech ;
  But women sometimes die of such a greed, —
Die for the small joys held beyond their reach,
  And the assurance they have all they need !

HIC JACET.

AND this is life : to live, to love, to lose !
  To feel a joy stir, like an unsung song,
The deep, unwrit emotions of our souls ;
Then, when we fain would utter it, to find
Our glad lips stricken dumb.

                              To watch a hope
Climb like a rising star, till from the heights
Of fair existence it sends lustre down,
Whose radiance makes earth's very shadows shine ;
Then suddenly to see it disappear,
Leaving a bleak, appalling emptiness
In all the sky it did illuminate.

To build up, stone by stone, a temple fair,
On whose white altars we do burn our days ;
To form its arches of our dearest dreams,
To shape its pillars of our strongest strength, —
Then suddenly to see that temple fall,
A broken and irreparable wreck,

Its shape all shapeless, and its formless form
In ruthless Ruin's unrelenting grasp.

To veil our shrinking eyes lest they should see
Life's grim appraisers, Death and Burial,
Come down the path that leads across our hearts,
And write us paupers in the Book of Love.

To dream, in all life's happy arrogance,
Life's proud proportions limitless, then to find
Life's limit narrowed down to one fresh grave ;
To stand beside that new-made mound and feel
Within that cell is locked forever up
The precious honey, gathered drop by drop
From out the fairest flower-fields of our souls ;
Lonely and desolate to cast ourselves,
In some White City of the Silent, down
Beside some cold, forbidding marble door,
And feel ourselves forever shut away
From that which was our dearest and our own ;
To know, however earnestly we knock,
That door will ne'er be opened unto us ;
To know the dweller there will never step
Beyond the boundary of that cruel gate ;
To know, howe'er we plead, no lip therein
Will break into its old accustomed smile.
The folded hands stretch out no welcomings,
The fastened eyelids never lift themselves
Again in answering anguish, or glad love,
From out the frozen bondage of their sleep.

8*   L

'T is this to love and bury out of sight
Some precious darling of our dearest years, —
Some far outstretching root of our own hearts,
Some flowery branch that we had hoped to train
Along the loftiest trellises of Hope.

Life, Love, and Loss! Three little words that make
The compass of that varied road which lies
Stretched out between our swaddles and our shroud!

Life, Love, and Loss! Three ripples on one brook:
Three widening branches of one mighty stream;
Three stemless currents. emptying themselves
Into one vast and vague Eternity!

TWO.

TO one he brought the rarest flowers
    That gold could buy,
And gave them with the courteous smile
    That masked a sigh.
Upon the other he bestowed,
    With scarce a look,
A few wild violets, gathered by
    A wayside brook.

When from the skies, that golden day,
    Went out the sun,
Of all the flowers the first received,
    Remained not one !
Some lured her swans ; some gayly graced
    The fawn she petted :
Some decked her starling's cage : all died,
    Not one regretted.

The other shyly from the world
    Turned her apart,
And hid her wayside violets
    Upon her heart.

And he who gave to each that day
  Such different share,
By one was scorned; the other breathed
  His name in prayer!

Years afterward, a woman died, —
  A lonely creature,
Whose sorrows were not written out
  On form or feature;
But they who shrouded her do say,
  Dead on her breast,
Close, close unto her cold dumb heart,
  Were violets pressed.

TO BE.

O DEATH ! wert thou only a journey to take,
Just a pilgrimage, whence to return by and by,
How many who boast of the happiest hearts,
From the world and its worry would turn them and die ;
In the realms of the resting rejoiced to sojourn, —
If they could but return, — if they could but return !

If we only could die for a day, or an hour,
And the tramp of our troubles could go on above
Our quieted hearts, which no longer would ache,
Nor break with their burdens of hate or of love, —
How sweet from existence thus briefly to sever,
Unawed by the awful Forever and Ever.

Not to sleep, but to die, — with no sense left awake,
Not a pulse left to thrill, not a nerve left to quiver, —
Then calmly to float out, uncaring, ungrieved,
Across the deep dark of the fathomless river ;
To tarry awhile, till the turn of the tide,
In the heavenly hush of the echoless side.

Could we lift a white finger and hail, when we would,
The mystical barge from the mystical shore,
What woes would we break from to beckon and wait,
O Death! for the undreaded dip of thy oar:
Glad to lay off our lives, as our robes are laid off,
Could we wear them again when but rested enough.

But it never has been, and it never can be;
We must weave out our lives to their uttermost end,
Let the warp and the woof be of iron or gold,
Wrought with roses that ravish, or thistles that rend;
And I would not be dead, like the dead in the grave,
Not for rest the profoundest that death ever gave:

For 't is sweet to exist, it is blessèd to be, —
To share of the sea, and the stars, and the sun,
To drink of the air, to exult in the light,
To be of the wonderful universe — One!
Though a shadow that lurks in life's valley beguiles
Our feet to press on to the Infinite Isles.

"ONE FOR YOU, AND ONE FOR ME."

"ONE for you, and one for me"—
　　Two lads under an orchard tree,
Counting the fruity favors cast
Down on the turf by last night's blast;
Yellow apple, and mellow pear,
And sunny peach, for each a share.
" One for you, and one for me " —
Truths not always the whole truth be.
The young cheeks blush, the young hearts stir;
" One for you, and one for me " —
　　And both for her !

" One for you, and one for me " —
Two youths stand where the waltzers be,
And watch the face of one fair girl
Float like a rose mid the rush and whirl.
To each she gives a word, a glance,
A witching smile, a promised dance ;
Then drifts the line of dancers down.
Two faces flush, two foreheads frown :
One mutters, " This no more shall be ; "
The other. " Not so equally
　　We stand with her !"

" One for you, and one for me "—
For each a chance, whate'er it be.
Two stern men, in a lonesome place.
Back to back from each other pace:
They halt — they wheel — a word — the ring
Of pistols hush the birds that sing!
Two gallant forms, both smitten. lie
Ten paces parted, sure to die.
" One for you, and one for me "—
How close the old days seem to be,
        With both for her!

" One for you. and one for me "—
Oh, reconciling memory,
That turns, with one sweet, magic breath,
To gold the iron chains of death!
" Lift me," said one.   " See, each forgives
The other, whilst that other lives."
E'en as he spoke, a marriage train
Swept down the road that crossed the plain,
And each saw in the fair young bride
The face of her for whom he died.
" Not for you, and not for me,"
The chilling lips breathed huskily,
        " And — both for her!"

FAREWELL TO MEXICO.

TRUE hearts, stanch friends, dear Mexico, farewell;
  Would I could pluck from my o'erflowing heart
Some rare bouquet of words whose depths might tell
What lips can speak not, nor these tears impart.
Between me and the shore the widening blue
Tells of the deepening seas to which I go;
From lessening barks floats back a faint " Adieu."
My soul replies — Farewell to Mexico!

I came a pilgrim to thy storied strand,
I go like one who into exile goes;
Surely I've found, in this enchanted land,
Some region where the fabled lotus grows.
I sigh not that so far across the deep
Fair Louisiana's orange-blossoms blow;
I only watch thy fading shores and weep.
Because I bid farewell to Mexico!

Bright picture-land! my thoughts, like trailing vines,
Wind back thy hills, thy vales, thy lakes along;
Cling round thine altars and thy ruined shrines,
And twine where mysteries and where memories throng.
Ye skies, in which resplendent sunsets burn,
Ye plains, ye palms, ye peerless peaks of snow!
From what rare realms of loveliness I turn
To sigh, and say — Farewell to Mexico!

Now faint and fainter grows the line of shore.
Upon our path springs the pursuing wind;
Our plunging prow tastes the blue brine once more,
While like a plume our white wake streams behind.
Like one last friend, proud Orizaba stands,
Against the sunset, 'neath his crown of snow:
We call aloud, we wave to him our hands;
He fails, he fades,— Farewell to Mexico!

ELEANOR.

ELEANOR, fair Eleanor!
   Dear, dainty, and delightful,
Of visions rare, of visions fair,
   My heart she renders quite full.
Not of to-day is her sweet way,
   Nor yester, nor to-morrow;
But from some epoch long by-gone
   Each charm she seems to borrow.

Eleanor, sweet Eleanor!
   I watch her winning graces,
And in my heart at once upstart
   Full twenty lovely faces
That hang in frames, with painters' names
   Attached, whose fame doth render
To fleeting beauty's mortal dower
   Their own immortal splendor.

Eleanor, quaint Eleanor!
  With high-heeled slippers ringing,
With manner meek, with patch on cheek,
  And netted workbag swinging —
A special charm — on rounded arm
  From elbow-sleeve out peeping,
With kerchief crossed on pointed waist,
  And paniered skirt down sweeping,—

Toward the chapel on the hill,
  This morn she stepped demurely:
" Some sketch unique from frame antique,"
  I said, " has wandered surely ! "
The buckles shone on shoe and zone,
  The dainty ruff rose starchly,
As 'neath her quaint poke-bonnet's brim
  She glanced me greeting archly.

Yonder, in that high-backed chair,
  Last night I saw her sitting,
Serenely sweet, in raiment neat,
  And busy with her knitting.
How quaint her dress, how smooth her tress,
  There in the old chair rocking,—
Intent, O cunning little maid,
  On toeing off a stocking !

Eleanor, wise Eleanor!
  Thus gracing her own graces,
She gains a dower of winsome power
  Denied more perfect faces.
Ah! even now, as her young brow
  Peeped from its old-time bonnet,
She seemed like modern music set
  To some mediæval sonnet.

Eleanor, rare Eleanor!
  A truce to idle rhyming;
Yet doth belong ofttimes to song
  Tones deeper than its chiming;
And, years untold, my heart will hold,
  With memories sweet to cherish,
Her image, quaintly picturesque,
  Too fair a thing to perish.

MY SOUL.

MY soul unto my heart did thus complain :
How long. O jailer, wilt thou here detain
    My restless spirit?
How long ere I may seek, in yonder skies,
The hallowed and the unconceived-of prize
    That souls inherit?

How long ere Time. the High-priest, comes to lay
His hand upon this dungeon door of clay
    And break its bars,
And set me free from mortal fears and feuds
To seek the grand and solemn solitudes
    Among the stars?

O heart, the heavenly spirit's earthly twin,
O mortal, locking the immortal in
    With human keys,
Have mercy ! Hide awhile thy watchful face,
And let my prisoned pinions fly to trace
    Eternities !

And yet, O tender, though most cruel heart,
I've much to thank thee for before we part,
   To rejoin never,
Ere Time's last billows I for aye have sounded,
Ere I the dim and misty cape have rounded
   Of the Forever!

I from life's clambering vines rich blooms have plucked,
And from its sweetest fruits my lips have sucked
   Delicious juices;
And I have quaffed that essence from above,
That only heavenly thing — pure, faithful Love —
   Which life produces.

The golden chalice of existence, lifted
High on the wave, into my grasp was drifted;
   Its luscious wine
In purple flow upon the beaker darkled,
And o'er the brim to lips athirsting sparkled
   In draughts divine!

In thy stern keeping I have grown the wings
Now fledged and pining for far nobler things,
   O guardian heart!
Too long I've fettered been to earth's cold floor,
I've loved and been beloved; there is no more —
   Now let us part.

I hear thee build the scaffold of my years,
Of sorrows, smiles, few hopes, and many fears,
   As days diminish;
I hear thy thick throbs fall like hammer blows,
Here muffled by a thorn, and there a rose, —
   When wilt thou finish?

When comes the hour, at midnight, dawn, or day,
When thou wilt draw these bolts and bars away
   With bated breath,
And ope for me the portals of this place,
And bid me that grim executioner face,
   Relentless Death?

Death, at whose hands we find our noblest birth;
Who frees us from the swaddling-clothes of earth
   And all its harms;
Who rocks the cradle of Eternity,
And lays us loving, grateful, glad, and free,
   In God's own arms!

SONNETS.

THE CHRISTENING.

I SAW the consecrated water fall,
   Unconscious boy, upon thy upturned brow;
I saw the solemn rites, I heard the vow
That swore to shelter thee from this world's thrall,
And aught of sin that might thy life engall.
E'en while the vow was uttered, saw I Care,
And Sorrow with his thorn-embroidered pall,
And siren-faced Temptation gathering there.
They said, "Though ye may love and guard this child,
Who is of earth must share of earthly dross;
Ye cannot keep him pure and undefiled.
Through us o'er trial he must triumph win;
We sign him with the sign of life's great cross,
That, knowing evil, he may shrink from sin."

9   M

MYSTERY.

AYE, all is mystery.   Not the skies alone,
    With their unfathomed secrecies of stars;
Nor science and religion with their wars;
Nor yet earth's lonely lands 'twixt zone and zone,
With hidden histories carved in voiceless stone:
But, too, sweet friendship that has left its scar
In passing, and the precious love that's gone
Out like a tide, and left us on the bar
Of bitterness, where bright waves come no more;
Ourselves, which to ourselves are mysteries;
The potent spark which speaks from shore to shore;
Creeds, which such hosts of cruel doubt involve;
Unbounded thought which through the boundless flies;
And life that problem we must die to solve.

THE WIND.

THE wind, that poet of the elements,
    To-night comes whistling down our tropic lanes,
And wakes the slumbrous hours with sweet refrains.
From creamy cups, filled with magnolia scents,
His luscious lips have gained rich recompense
For scaling her green towers. To him complains
The lonesome lily of her discontents,
While orange-blossoms scent the Southern lanes.
The jasmine, with her white soul in her face,
Bestows her holy kisses on his mouth ;
Before the pilgrim-minstrel violets place
The purple censers of their fervent youth ;
And nodding poppies, with a drowsy grace,
Anoint his feet with dream-oils of the South.

DON'T YOU REMEMBER?

I.

ROAMING among the daisies, you and I,
　　The tangled drifts of daisies, glad and young,
Beneath the azure of a cloudless sky,
The zephyrs catching, as they wander by,
　　The tender accents falling from your tongue —
　　　　　　　　　　Don't you remember?

II.

A country glow upon my girlish cheek,
　　As side by side the wooded slopes we rise,
Or in the fresh spring mould the beech-sprouts seek,
Or part the rushes by the winding creek,
　　Reading sweet secrets in each other's eyes —
　　　　　　　　　　Don't you remember?

III.

The soft wind tossing back my light brown hair,
　　The robins building in the apple-trees;
A scent of roses on the morning air,
The birth of buds about us everywhere,
　　A warm and tender gladness on the breeze —
　　　　　　　　　　Don't you remember?

IV.

The brook that leaped adown the mountain height
And sped away, nor ever looked behind,
As if it feared the stern old mountain might
Find out the secret of its hasty flight,
    And follow on its truant feet to bind —
                Don't you remember?

V.

The hills we climbed through merry baths of dew
    To catch the sun's light on our beaming faces,
Ere he might cast his beams on hearts less true
Than yours to me, Love, or than mine to you,
    Wasting the treasure of his first embraces —
                Don't you remember?

VI.

The stream meandering through the vale below,
    The marshy meadow's reedy banks between,
Where the coquettish cowslips flirted so
With every breeze, or bent their bright lips low
    And kissed the water from their beds of green —
                Don't you remember?

VII.

The bit of river southward of the town,
    Pale in the dawn, like some gray lock of hair
That Winter might have clipped from his old crown,
And given to Spring, to keep when he was gone,
    In kindly memory of him to wear —
                Don't you remember?

VIII.

The pollard willow, where the honey-bees
   Gave concerts in the branches all day long;
The blackbirds whistling in the hickory-trees;
The bobolink on a milkweed in the breeze,
   Almost committing suicide with song —
                              Don't you remember?

IX.

The fallen petals by the fruit trees given
   To drape with white the emerald robes of May,
Along the country lanes and roadsides driven,
As if some young bride in her flight to Heaven
   Her bridal wreath had scattered on the way —
                              Don't you remember?

X.

The bloodroot that came up with such a shriek
   Whene'er we pulled it from its hiding-places;
The plants and mosses that we used to seek,
While Earth with her rent bosom could not speak,
   But as we robbed her breathed hard in our faces —
                              Don't you remember?

XI.

The old beech woods upon the hillsides steep,
   Where the wild honeysuckle always grew;
Fair golden harvests that you loved to reap,
Sweet golden harvests that I loved to keep,
   Blessed by the sunshine and baptized with dew —
                              Don't you remember?

XII.

The quaint old garden with its gravelled walks,
  Its grass-plots starred with golden dandelions,
Its daffodils, May-pinks, and hollyhocks,
Its white syringa with sweet-smelling stalks,
  And neighbors coming after slips and scions —
                    Don't you remember?

XIII.

There 'neath my chin you held the buttercup,
  Some truth you saucily declared to prove :
Then cried, when bashfully my eyes would droop,
" A girl's blush is the flag her heart runs up
  To signal its surrender unto Love ! " —
                    Don't you remember?

XIV.

And then you clasped my brown hand in your own ;
  You know how wilfully you could persist ;
There was a strange new music in your tone,
Thrilling and sweet, — well, we were all alone,
  I may mistake, but — were my lips not kissed? —
                    Don't *you* remember?

XV.

Then how the village bells rang out one day,
  How joyfully we two walked side by side ;
The church door opened and we knelt to pray,
Friends crowded round their kindly words to say,
  And shake our hands, and some one called me *bride* —
                    Don't you remember?

XVI.

Our bark since then has touched on many strands ;
  Our wandering feet have roamed in many climes,
Our brows been kissed by suns of far-off lands ;
New friends, dear Love, have clasped our willing hands,
  But the old times, the ever dear old times —
          We both remember !

ANGÉLE.

HOW didst thou rest, dear Love, last night
In thy narrow, narrow bed?
Was the young rose quiet that, waxen white,
Kept watch by thy hidden head,
Angéle!
Watch by thy hidden head?

What did the cypress say to thee
As it drooped by thy young feet?
Did it tell thee, darling, it stood for me,
And bid thee to slumber sweet,
My Love!
Bid thee to slumber, Sweet?

My heart an oak was, long ago,
And it wore an evergreen crown;
And the hallowed mistletoe, Love, wert thou
That into its life had grown:
But Death,
The druid, cut thee down!

9*

Now has my heart forgot its strength,
    And forgot its sturdy pride ;
And my life a dream is of dreary length,
    With thee unto it denied,
        Angéle !
      Thee unto it denied.

All night I strode the cold sea beach ;
    And the waves came groping there,
For a treasure wailing beyond their reach
    With an unavailing prayer,
        Dear Love !
      Wild, unavailing prayer.

Had they not chilled thy bosom white,
    And exulted o'er thy charms,
And then cast thee forth to the outer night
    From satiate, kindless arms, —
        Poor child !
      Careless and cruel arms?

Had they not bruised thy forehead fair,
    And betrayed thy tender cheek,
And the sea-weeds twisted into thy hair,
    And stifled thy dying shriek, —
        O Love !
      Stifled thy dying shriek?

The salt sea spray leaps up again
  To this breast unto thee denied ;
How I curse each billow that dares profane
  The brow thou hast sanctified,
      Angéle !
    Kissed, and so sanctified.

I hear the poniards of the rain,
  As they stab the earth in sleep ;
But they cannot smite thee back to thy pain, —
  I buried thee down too deep,
      Angéle !
    Buried thee down too deep.

Beneath the muffling moss and grass
  They may slide, and cringe, and creep ;
And the under roots of thy cypress pass,
  But cannot disturb thy sleep,
      Lost one !
    Cannot disturb thy sleep.

Though swift they slip, and hide perchance
  Where thy gleaming headboard stands,
They can never into thy young face glance,
  They cannot unfold thy hands,
      Angéle !
    Poor little folded hands.

· The rain ! 't is on my forehead yet, —
    For my feet there is no rest ;
And the skies are dark with a dull regret ;
    They 've drowned the moon in the west, —
        Ah me !
    Drowned the moon in the west.

Didst sleep, my Love, the whole night long
    With thy white hands on thy breast,
And the fresh young lilies thy locks among,
    As when thou wert laid to rest,
        Fair girl !
    Tenderly laid at rest?

All night was thy sweet sleep profound,
    Was thy clinging shroud unstirred,
Was thy slim grave undisturbed by a sound, —
    No echoes of anguish heard,
        Angéle !
    Echoes of anguish heard?

The rosebuds in thy fingers prest,
    Did they dare, dear Love, to die ?
They were buried alive upon thy breast, —
    I envy them as they lie,
        Beloved !
    Where it were bliss to die.

Yet falls the drear. unpitying rain ;
  And the lips of night are pale,
As they kiss. on yon tumultuous main,
  The wings of the passing gale,
      Dear one !
    Stormy wings of the gale.

All night I strode the beaten beach,
  Where the waves knelt prone and pale,
With their white lips moaning, in broken speech,
  Thy name, my beloved Angéle,
      Thy name !
    Moaning for thee. Angéle.

They sought my life, the billows blue,
  And I did not stand apart ;
There is no more harm that a foe can do
  When he has broken the heart,
      Dear one !
    Broken a loving heart.

The tempest rode the whirling world,
  And the sea arose in might ;
And I rushed where billows the blackest swirled,
  And bade them my life to smite, —
      Ha ! Ha !
    Vainly I bade them smite !

Why, thou hast left thy grave, Angéle !
And thy shroud floats on the deep ;
There it beckons to me — ah ! why so pale?
My darling ! couldst thou not sleep, —
Not sleep?
Couldst thou not from me sleep?

Thy tresses drip with ocean damps,
And thy dear lips, do they move?
All the lamps are out in night's golden camps,
But never the lamps of love,
Angéle !
Quenchless are lamps of love.

I thought thee prone, like some young nun,
All at peace in her lone cell ;
On thy breast a cross, all thy penance done, —
Who dared to dissolve the spell
Of sleep,
Kissing thy eyelids down?

The black locks of the swart queen Night
Are all trailing on the sea ;
But they cannot veil thee out of my sight,
With little hands stretched to me,
My Love !
Little hands stretched to me.

Weird voices answer from the shore
　　To the shout of storm-lost waves,
And the solemn pines with sympathant roar
　　Respond from the forest naves,
　　　　And chant, —
　.　Chant, like exultant braves!

What phosphorescent gleam now plays
　　Where the crested waters sweep?
Ha! the billows burn with the frenzied gaze
　　Of eyes that no more will sleep, —
　　　　Eyes doomed
　　　Never again to sleep!

Thy grave is empty! From the night
　　I can hear thee calling me ;
And each billow's crest is a beacon light
　　To guide me afar to thee,
　　　　My Own!
　　　Guide me afar to thee.

Oh, wait! Angéle, fear not the dark,
　　And fear not the tempest's breath!
I will come to thee in a swift, lone bark,
　　Steered by the helmsman Death,
　　　　Angéle!
　　　Wait, and fear not the dark!

THE SPECTRE'S BRIDAL.

A SKELETON once ran away with a ghost, —
   Oh, the graveyard wall it was high and damp! —
But no sentinel's challenge of "Who goes there?"
   Rung down o'er the dead in their marble camp.
So they clambered high, and they clambered low,
And never a corpse turned over to throw
From his mouldering eyes a forbidding stare,
To check the flight of this singular pair.

The skeleton, he had lain quiet for years
   In his handsome coffin of precious wood,
Maintaining a dignified attitude there,
   Just as a virtuous skeleton should.
The ghost had belonged to a beautiful maid,
Left here by herself only yesterday, dead, —
She who never before had anywhere gone
Without some respectable *chaperon*.

They buried her here, in her fresh, sweet youth,
   Like a flower that we put away to press,
With a lingering look and a tender touch,
   In the first bright bloom of its loveliness,

And here she was now, by a young man's side, —
Young, for he ceased to grow old when he died ;
And, although he was heartless, his gallant bones
Were moved at the sight of the girl's tombstones.

And that giddy young ghost, she could n't keep still ;
 The coffin was close, and the grave was so damp !
And how could she judge of the fit of her shroud,
 Or the style of her *coiffure*, without any lamp?
The courteous skeleton, lying next door,
Dismayed, heard the ghost her sad trials deplore ;
And, though hitherto quite resigned to his fate,
He now felt impelled *to articulate.*

He struggled to sit, and he struggled to stand ;
 But his joints would n't work, and his limbs felt queer :
" I declare, I 've grown loose in my habits," he said,
 " Though my habits were ' fast' when I came to sleep
  here."
He wriggled his jaws, and he nodded his head ;
His long folded fingers he cautiously spread ;
Then with one supreme effort stepped out in the air :
The ghost of the girl he found already there.

The slender moon lay in the summery sky
 Like the paring of somebody's great thumb-nail.
And, under its shining. the skeleton looked,
 To the pretty young ghost, rather mouldy and stale.

The meeting was awkward in many respects, —
As seems very natural, if one reflects, —
For the ghost's taste in dress could now naught avail her,
And the skeleton was not right fresh from his tailor.

They stood in Death's horrible kingdom of Hush,
    By his dungeons of dumbness, cold, dreary, and deep;
While, ripe on night's mystical prairies above,
    Grew the harvest of stars which the morning would
        reap;
And meteors — fire-laden argosies — sailed
The gulfs of the air, where no passing voice hailed
To question whence came they, or where were they
        bound.
O'er the oceans of space in the silence profound.

And yonder, and yonder, and yonder revealed,
    Were unlimited realms for unlimited flight.
Well, what could that ghost and that skeleton do?
    Like some mortals, the two fell in love at first sight.
They stood there alone, and the skeleton saw
That here was his chance for no mother-in-law!
For the rest? Opportunity forms the base
Of most of the sins of the human race.

There were none to consult with regard to each other, —
    The ghost quite forgot to ask. Was he rich?
He did not inquire if her dear great-grandfather
    Made candles, or soap, or had known how to stitch.

She felt too light-headed for cavil or question ;
He felt too polite to make any suggestion ;
And both, perhaps, felt how awkward 't would be
For either to climb up a family-tree !

So joined they their hands, these two innocent spectres,
　　Nor vowed they such vows as are blest from above ;
They talked not of loving till "death do us sever,"
　　But swore, " naught shall sever us while we both love."
Remember, the maid was a very young woman, —
A maiden's first lover oft seems superhuman ;
And as for that skeleton, — well, 't was not odd he
Should say to himself that the ghost was no-body.

Their kisses were pure as the pure polar ice,
　　And as bloodless and cold as a toad's foot at noon ;
And misty and chill was their strange wedding-ring,
　　For it was the wide ring that encircled the moon.
Much talking there was not, for mere lack of tongues ;
Much sighing there was not, for mere lack of lungs ;
But the wedding went on, without prayer, without priest,
Without altar, or organ, or favor, or feast.

Then the skeleton climbed, and the ghost she soared ;
　　Over graves of the "oldest and best" they groped ;
But the beds lay deep, and they slept so sound,
　　Not a slumberer found out the pair had eloped.

Not one marble door slid out of its place ;
Not one woman lifted a peering face ;
For comfort, go purchase a graveyard " share," —
The neighbors all mind their own business there.

Up, over the wall, where the whole night long
    All slimy and sleepy the green lizards hide,
Beyond the grim gates of the Garden of Graves,
    The skeleton hurries his ghostly young bride.
Up, up, o'er the roofs of the slumbering town ;
On, on, where the river goes hurrying down, —
'T was the oddest sight in the world, I 'm sure,
This bridegroom and bride on their wedding tour.

The owl on her branch of an old hollow tree
    Uplifted her lids at a sight so new,
And ruffled her feathers, and hooted aloud
    Her impudent query, " To whoo?   To whoo?
As onward they sped, and a dew of affright
Stood out on the face of the startled night.
And the white little moon slipped under a cloud.
At the gleam of the young woman's wedding shroud.

And somebody says that the Yucca rang out
    That night from its tower of pallid bells,
As the pair went by. a chime that seemed
    Half wedding marches, half funeral knells ;
And the tall green cane and the nodding rice
Bowed down but once, though they shivered thrice,

As over them sped, most horribly human,
This frame of a man and this ghost of a woman!

How vast their domain in the regions of space!
　How starry their night-times, their mornings how sunny.
Whilst they dine on that bliss we poor mortals know well.
　A course of true love, and for dessert no money!
Though she had her own stage of existence, this bride,
The couple were never once known to ride;
But from furtherest star to earth's furtherest ocean,
They travelled content with their own locomotion!

They have their own sport, such as suiteth them best!
　When we shrink at the shriek of the wind, sometimes,
'T is only the skeleton whistling a tune
　He is trying to set to his pretty wife's rhymes!
To ocean they carry the dangerous breeze
That startles the sailor with suddening seas,
And who has not heard, mid the tempest's wild battle,
The skeleton's fingers his window-sash rattle?

And oft, when we lie on our pillows and quake
　At the sound of the shutters that clatter so loud,
'T is only the skeleton scurrying by,
　With a rattle of bones and the swish of a shroud.
Up, over the roof of my silent bedchamber,
I often and oft do hear the two clamber,
With footsteps that are not of earth or of air,
Yet are here, and are yonder, and everywhere.

Their honeymoon? Heaven knows how that was spent!
  There's a watering-place, maybe, somewhere in the
    clouds,
For a bride and a groom whose outfits consist
  Of nothing else under the moon but their shrouds!
The current expenses, we know, of this pair
Could not have been much, since they lived upon air :
As many young pairs, more romantic than prudent,
Have lovingly tried to, but found that they could n't!

They were happy? Of course! She never had servants,
  He never was known to stay out late at night ;
She ran up no bills, he ran no fast horses ;
  She had no dressmaker, he never got " tight."
They lived a most joyous Bohemian life,
This skeleton grim and his airy young wife ;
He thinks that a bride is a " light weight" to carry,
She thinks a dead girl is a fool not to marry.

And so, hand in hand, from the dawn unto dawn,
  Knowing well in each other their happiness lies,
They wander mid nebulæ, star-dust, and moons,
  Two jubilant gypsies that camp in the skies.
Such a bridegroom and bride seem rather absurd,
But of matches as odd we have all of us heard ;
And, if we but think of it, man, at the most,
Is only a skeleton wed to a ghost.

NEXT YEAR.

THIS afternoon, as through the fields we strolled,
   Our shadows, side by side, went on before,
As though the path, beneath our feet unrolled,
   Two dusky guides went forward to explore.
Our way was mid the honey haunts of bees,
   Past scented, hay-ripe meadow-lands, and where,
In streams, by mill-wheels lashed to mimic seas,
   The weeping willow laved her lavish hair.
Thy lip was laughing, and thine eye was clear —
" Remember me," thou saidst, " this time next year."

Birds, gayly winged, like painted shuttles, shot
   Now in, now out, among the summer leaves ;
Oft with her woofs — stray threads her loom has caught —
   Unconscious Nature mortal destinies weaves.
The softened sunshine sifted through the trees ;
   Mosaicked light and shadow 'neath us lay ;
The gurgling stream, the voices of the bees,
   To perfect music set the perfect day ;
While I, beside thee, eager bent to hear
Thee say, " Remember me this time next year."

Next year!   What words I spoke — what answer thou!
    Why should I strive those spectres to recall?
Suffice it, down the ways that thou wilt go,
    By thine my shadow nevermore will fall.
The scented summer-time will come again,
    With busy beaks the birds be building here,
The meadows be as sweet, as ripe the grain,
    The brooks as brown as now, " this time next year;"
While I afar shall feel thy path I bless,
Since thus that path will know one shadow less.

EMBRYO.

I FEEL a poem in my heart to-night,
    A still thing growing ;
As if the darkness to the outer light
    A song were owing :
A something strangely vague, and sweet, and sad,
    Fair, fragile, slender ;
Not tearful, yet not daring to be glad,
    And oh, so tender !

It may not reach the outer world at all,
    Despite its growing ;
Upon a poem-bud such cold winds fall
    To blight its blowing.
But, oh, whatever may the thing betide,
    Free life or fetter,
My heart, just to have held it till it died,
    Will be the better !

THE PRINTING-PRESS.

GOD said, " Let there be light." Lo ! at his word,
Back from the dome profound, the velvet veil
Of darkness swiftly swept, " and there was light."

From chaos wrought, the perfect Earth awoke,
Thrilled to her depths, and her perfection knew ;
Each welcoming atom its completeness felt,
And the first sun-flood fell upon the world.

The primal Morn came with her opulent arms,
From which, o'erfalling, dropped delightful down
The fructifying rays, the joy of warmth,
The sweet surprise of color.   Fragrance and Shade,
Like loving sisters, in green valleys smiled,
And from the purple mists the hills arose
And gazed appalled across each other's shoulders.
'Neath the concentred splendors of the orb
That burned above them its miraculous fires,
Primeval forests quickened into life,
And their white blood began its circulant course.

Deep in its dungeon lay the tiny seed;
A sunbeam with transfiguring touch fell there,
And lo! a germ of forests yet to be!
The lowliest weed that late had lain asleep,
Worthless and chill on the benumbèd soil,
Became at once a tome, on which was writ
The law as on the giants of creation.

Upon their trembling petals roses felt
The warm kiss of Omnipotence, and breathed
Responsive sweetness.
                      Stately palms upheld
Adoring branches.   Perfect lilies raised
Their silver cups, and drank in new perfection.
The rocks, the plains, the everlasting seas,
Stirred to their centres.
                      The creature learned the law
Creation made for him.   Beasts roamed the wood;
In the first gardens sang the first glad birds;
The waters became vital; fields grew fair;
Blossoms assumed new dyes, the sky new tints,
The heights new grandeur.   Life was in the world.

From out abysmal space Night stole, and threw
Her strange and sombre shadow over all;
And from the hollow of her dusky hand
Flung darkness back upon the sea and shore.

" Let there be light," God said, " and there was light."

From luminous fountains of the sky it poured
In tempered torrents of effulgence down.
From wide horizon to horizon rolled
Stupendous constellations.   Orion's belt
Gleamed where the mighty hunter stood on high,
And held his trophies in the glare of suns
Fresh from Creation's hand.

                          The white stars burst
Into eternal blossom.   Unknown spheres
At mystic altars of the Infinite
Kindled their never quenching fires, and swung
To their supernal orbits.
                          The asteroids
Clung like a flock of frightened birds unto
The azure empyrean.   Helmeted Mars
Stood with his lurid visor up, and dared
Defiant worlds.
                          Planets took up their march
In swift obedience to the silent laws,
And went their way flinging through boundless space,
From never empty lamps, perpetual light.

Suns and their satellites their radiance blent
With grand celestial mysteries, yet kept
A secret from the earth.
                          The Southern Cross
Hurled its red jewels on the astral deep,
And left them there to glow forevermore.
From stellar silences young Lyra looked,

And the sidereal Scorpion grandly stretched
Across the shining skies his luminous length.

Filled with a sudden glory, lesser orbs
Flashed down the dizzying heights their lambent rays,
Trembling to find themselves so glorious.

Slender with youth, the primogenial moon
Her golden hammock in the zenith hung,
And, swaying in the far refulgent fields,
Shot scintillant arrows over land and sea.

In clustered splendor on the sapphire heights,
Complete in lustrous numbers, smiled afar
The Pleiadean sisters.

Over all,
Resplendent, hung the unmeasured Milky Way, —
A bridge of worlds, arched over countless worlds ;
And drowned lay darkness in the drenching light.

Earth was ; Light was ; Man was : and all the world
Thrilled to the harmonies of Genesis.

The moon and stars and sun shone on. Light was :
Through change and counterchange it lived unchanged ;
Still was there heard a voice crying aloud,
" Let there be light !—yea, yea ! let there be light !"
It was a voice that issued from men's souls,

From hearts that burned with deep, ambitious fires,
With yearnings vague, and indeterminate wants.

The nations of the earth took up the cry :
Men wrought, and delved, and builded monuments.
They made the stars their books, and from them drew
Portent and inspiration.   Invention rose
And flourished in the land.   Science was great ;
And Architecture, with luxurious hand,
Inwrought her temples with rare ivories,
And sate her palaces on precious stones.

Cities sprang up on many a verdant site :
Palmyra's pillars gemmed the Assyrian plain ;
The ships of Tarshish bore the dyes of Tyre,
Odorous freight of precious cedar wood,
And spices from the famed Phœnician coast,
Toward the palaces of Solomon.

Damascus shone beneath the Syrian sun ;
And, great within her hundred brazen gates,
Where mid the hanging gardens proudly rose
The haughty grandeur of Semiramis,
Sat towered Babylon.
                                    Persepolis
Became the pride and " glory of the East,"
.And by the Murdusht meadows builded up
Her temples, tombs, and marble monuments.
Kingdoms and kings ruled and were overruled :
Egypt, and proud Assyria, and Chaldea,

The classic three, rose to their height in power,
Then toppled to the deep and echoing tomb
Of mighty things that were.
            The bearded scribe
Sculptured the stone, or traced with patient hand
The labored page of the papyrus leaf
Graved with the stylus, or, in precious inks
Of fluent metals, dipped the Nilotic reed.

Meanwhile from crumbling places tottered down
The bricks of Babylon, with the cuneiform
Inscriptions of dead heroes and great kings.

From peak to peak of the vast centuries
Time slowly stepped. Creed after creed was born,
And swept in turn from off the face of earth.
From him who was King Suddhodana's son,
To him in gardens of Gethsemane,
Men turned, and hungered, and were fed, and drank
The subtle essence of Divinity, —
Were strong, were sad, were humble, were rejoiced,
Grew great with earth's best greatness in their lives,
And passed to death with fortitude sublime.
Yet from their burial-places came the Voice,
Calling from what was not, " Let there be light!"

As in the earliest moments of the morn
A tender radiance gives sweet hints that Dawn
Is smiling at the Orient's shining gates,
So came a strange yet penetrating gleam

Across the mental shadows of the time,
And, flickering in the Orient of men's hopes,
Stole toward an ancient city on the Rhine,
And entered at the stony gates of Mainz.

It wandered past the famous Eichelstein,
Past Roman ruins where the imperial hand
Of Charlemagne its lasting impress left ;
Traversed the crooked streets and narrow ways ;
Went out among the roofs, the lofty towers,
The homes and altars of the quaint old town.
It hovered o'er the pillow of the priest ;
It glittered past the scholar and the sage ;
It turned from luxury's couch and pride's demands,
And entered where, within his lowly room,
An eager artisan bent above his work
With busy fingers and fast-beating heart.
Here stayed the ray, and dropped its light divine
Upon the earnest brow of Gutenberg.

Beneath its radiance Genius recognized
Her child, and with a kindling kiss woke all
The latent fires within his eager soul.
'Neath that inspiring touch his hand became
The chosen instrument to set the torch
Of quenchless progress on Time's mighty gates.

As from the seed the generous verdure grows
To glad the earth, — as from the acorn spring

The lordly forests holding in their depths
The ships of commerce and the wheels of war,
The food to fill the ravenous mouths of steam,
Traffic's broad roads, and cities yet unbuilt, —
So that white ray that fell on Rhenish Mainz,
And rested there four hundred years ago,
Was the small spark from which has grown apace
A lustre, searching and far reaching, shed
Upon remotest corners of the globe.
Then it illumed a set of wooden blocks;
Now, from ten million million fonts of type,
It glitters in the firmament of Time.

'T is light, which grows as grows the banyan-tree;
Each slender branch becomes in turn a root,
Each root again sends up its flexile branch,
Till one perpetual range of vigorous growth,
Whose limits mortal man may not assign,
Marks its unending march around the world.

As some far sun astronomers have found,
Whose burnished rays, like plummets, were cast down,
In the beginning, through the seas of space, —
Rays which must fall through ages yet to come,
Sounding eternities on their way to meet
The gaze of races still unborn. — even so
Must spread the vivid, permeating beams
Of that great light John Gutenberg discerned
In thought's broad universe, the PRINTING-PRESS.

The king it is that stands behind all thrones,
With power boundless as the realms of space;
In one firm hand the lamp of knowledge burns,
The other, reason's flambeau holds aloft,
And the twin flames illuminate the world.

There is no good it cannot multiply;
No wrong its brow august cannot frown down.
Religion, politics, morals, and the law
Are fagots in its fingers to light men
With kindling beacons to exalted heights,
Or point the lurid depths of evil out.
Progress and Education stand upon
Its right hand and its left, and round them falls
This light that makes them known to all mankind:
It beckons bygone ages near, until
They stand so close who reads the present needs
But turn the page, and lo! the past is there.
It folds the parted corners of the earth
Together as a scroll, and at men's hearths
The arctic snows and tropic blossoms meet,
And Occident and Orient clasp hands.

It throws its light on Famine's bleeding lips,
And toward her Plenty's generous footstep guides;
Lorn Ignorance, grovelling in her sloth and want,
It gently leads to Wisdom's noble hand.

Like the fair tent of which the fable tells,
Whose magic folds could hide a mustard-seed,

Or so expand as to conceal the earth, —
So does the Press, from simple A B C —
The mustard-seed of knowledge, taught beside
The first, best schoolroom, the fond mother's knee —
Expand its folds until it covers all
Of learning, science, literature, and art.

With a magician's power, its magic light
Men's names upon immortal canvas writes,
And lifts them to the gaze of all the world.
Long since Fame came, and in its gleams laid down
Her brazen trump. There humbled Jove beheld
Such thunderbolts as he had never dared
To hurl from heights of old Olympus down.
From the deep waters of oblivion
It rescues drowning Genius. Through its might
We seem to hear again on Grecian hills
The eloquent accents of Demosthenes.
The Forum's echoes once again awake
With Cæsar's voice and Cicero's ringing tones ;
While Miriam's cymbals and sweet David's psalms
Reverberate adown the centuries.

Itself an orator whose tongue the gods
Have touched with living fire, its luminous words,
Day after day, with never tiring zeal,
Flash over hemisphere and hemisphere.
'T is the inspired preacher who goes forth
To " preach the gospel unto all the world," —
The golden gospel of enlightenment.

Men look back from a world of printed books,
Upon a world with but ONE printed book.
Progress triumphant waves o'er Then and Now
Her radiant banner; and the darkness grows
Alight, as night grows luminous with stars ;
While what men name as light quivers upon
The verge of greater light to come, until
The soul, unveiled, the splendor of the rays
Scarce dares to face.

                The scribe has laid away
His ancient reed and his papyrus leaf
As relics, whereunto research will turn,
And reverential learning burn its lamp,
In dusty chambers of antiquity.
The bricks of Babylon to the scholar's hand
Yield slowly up their mystic lettered lore ;
And while one to the patient seeker gives
The half-light of its shadowed history,
From continent to continent the Press
Has flashed its rays and met them around the globe !

I looked across a monumented land.
On every side I saw defiant stone
And many-metaled bronze, with sculptured names
Of heroed greatness in their guardianship.
I said, " Where, in commemorative clay,
In glittering marble or in shining brass,
On this broad land is reared the towering shaft
Whose carving chisels have immortal grown
By contact with the name of GUTENBERG?

Its crest," I said, " must be among the skies ;
Its base must lie upon the world's wide centre,
And all the nations must thereto have brought,
In grateful tribute, gold and precious stones,
To build it up with radiance to outshine
The famed Ephesian dome, or palaces
Which had for their foundations priceless gems."

Last night an answer came to me in dreams ;
It said, " Such monument hath Gutenberg
As never rose to mortal man before !
Each corner of its dazzling base is laid
On each of the four corners of the earth.
Its summit rises where the finite eye
Of man is blinded by Infinity.
There hath the veiléd Past her treasures poured ;
Thereon the Future sheds her brightest smile ;
Tradition has bestowed her gathered lore,
And meek Religion brought her shining cross ;
The poet there has placed his wreath of bays ;
The sage, the jewels of his wisdom borne ;
Commerce, rare trophies from the land and sea ;
Science and Learning, all their treasured store ;
Music, her most ; the Beautiful, its best.

" There all the sacred Nine have tribute poured ;
And Intellect, Culture, and Refinement stand,
With hearts inlocked, beside the ascending shaft ;
While Genius bows a reverential front,
As Progress there his sealéd orders brings.

The royal hands of married Steel and Steam
Bear day by day new treasures to the spot
Where, grander than earth's grandest monuments,
Rises this dome of domes, the PRINTING-PRESS.
And as of old the Parsee's quenchless flame
Burned by the altar and the sacred hearth,
So burn the fervid fires of Eloquence
Beside this vast and universal shrine
At which the nations of the world bow down,
And where, on high, Art's loving hand hath traced
The immortal name, — JOHANNES GUTENBERG."

University Press : John Wilson and Son, Cambridge.